A Mur___ __ Crows

Barry Dobey

Contents.

1

Witnesses to Atrocities

After the failed takeover of the Square, Don Mason had led Cynthia
Dodds, Amanda Blewitt and Sharon Thompson back to the gate, 'None of
you can stay and I warn you against returning to Millfield, I haven't
finished there. Donaldson's supplies are ours now. If I see any of you
again, I'll kill you.'

Cynthia Dodds was pleading for Don to let them stay. She knew they
wouldn't last long out there. Dead were appearing from up the front street
and from the entrance to Millfield. A lot of dead.

Will Masters, the young man who had spent every day, since the
outbreak, searching for orphaned children, in Bedlington, was right, when
he'd earlier warned them that the shooting had attracted the attention of the
undead.

The gate closed and locked behind the three women and the they stood on
the pavement and looked around them. There were dead making their way
down the front street adjacent to the Black Bull pub, a large group were
descending the slope onto the main road from Millfield and a group
appeared out from the road into Hollymount Avenue, no doubt and as Will
had said, attracted to the sound of gun shots earlier.

Cynthia was holding Sharon's hand. Sharon had been watching through
the storehouse window when her husband, Craig was decapitated by
Dowser's son, Paul Dawson. She was still in shock and unresponsive.
Cynthia could feel Sharon trembling. Her hand was ice cold.

Amanda looked around and quickly crossed the road, 'follow me, our
only chance is to head back for Millfield. I know he warned us not to, but
if we stay out in the open, we're dead. I know somewhere, come on.'
Cynthia led Sharon across the road and the three passed through the alley
between the front row of Millfield Court and La Torre Restaurant, that was
once the Millfield pub. They stopped at the end of the alley and waited for
two dead to make their way out of sight and then they ran down towards
Millfield.

Amanda looked over her shoulder as they ran, 'be quick, you two, there's only one way out of here. There'll be dead in the alley behind, by now. They saw us cross the road and it's a dead end back that way.'

There were still around ten dead, slowly making their way out of Millfield, towards the street, so the three women kept low, making their way past them, behind parked cars.

As they passed Millfield East, they could see their houses, partly boarded up with wooden pallets, but they could see a path had been made between, so people had been inside.

Amanda pointed to the entrance to Millfield, from Church lane. It had been badly blocked by cars, but easily passed. Amanda spoke again, 'we need to get across there, third house in. It was where Alec hung out. Gary told me he's seen him go in there. Alec kept a key under a planter. Hopefully it's still there. We'll have to make a run for it, though. There're dead passing our houses. If we run along the opposite side, we should get to Alec's hang out, before they cut us off. Find the key and we're safe. It's our only chance.'

Four dead were walking past their abandoned houses, when they made a run along the opposite side of the grass field, past the Ashford's house, where days earlier, the gang had murdered the whole family and left baby Amelia for dead.

They were heard and spotted immediately by the dead, who about turned and crossed onto the overgrown field and made their way towards them.

Cynthia was almost dragging Sharon along and Amanda made it to the house about twenty yards in front of her. There were around ten small ceramic planters in a line along the wall and she frantically, one after the other, threw them to the side.

The dead were nearing, as Cynthia and Sharon got to the door. Amanda was frantic, 'the key isn't here, shit! Fucking shit!' The four dead had reached the gate and Cynthia closed it against the latch and retreated, but it was a low gate and garden wall, so the dead fell over and into the garden.

As the dead were getting back to their feet, Cynthia looked at the planters, strewn across the path. The key was stuck to mud on the bottom of one of them. She ran over and grabbed the key and ran back to the front door. The dead were on their feet, only a few yards away. Cynthia's hand was shaking so much, she couldn't hit the keyhole. Amanda quickly took it out of her hand, put the key in the door and fell into the house.

Cynthia grabbed Sharon at the same time as one of the dead reached for her. It had grabbed her pullover. As the other dead converged around her, Cynthia grabbed the bottom of Sharon's pullover and pulled it up over her head. The dead man fell back, pullover in hand and Sharon and Cynthia fell the other way, into the house. Amanda slammed the door closed and the other three dead simultaneously bumped against it.

The three women made their way into the kitchen, Cynthia quickly checking the back door was locked.

Sharon sat down at the kitchen table. She was sobbing, inconsolably and shaking with fear. Cynthia sat beside her and cuddled her in, 'let me check, were you bit?' Sharon mumbled, 'no, no, I don't think so.'

Cynthia checked Sharon over. She was still grieving her own husband, Sammy, who had been shot by Ian Clark, while looting Dene View, but she had been lucky enough not to have witnessed this, particularly lucky in the sense Sammy was still alive when the dead had converged on him and Abe Gardener, that day, condemned to be eaten alive for the gang's murder of Ian Clarke's wife, Maeve.

Cynthia put her hand on Sharon's cheek, 'no bites, you'll be ok, Sharon.' 'We can't stay here long, but it will buy us a bit of time.' Amanda Blewitt was amazingly calm, bearing in mind she had just nearly been eaten by the dead and she'd earlier seen her husband, Gary shot dead by Don Mason. She looked out of the kitchen window into the overgrown back garden.

The four dead had made their way into the back garden and were looking around and listening, heads on their sides. She stepped back from the window and watched, as they wandered around the garden, then made their way back towards the front of the house.

Amanda went through to the sitting room, slightly pulled aside the curtain and watched as the four dead stumbled over the wall and gate and made their way down Millfield.

'They're gone, we're safe for now.' Amanda went back into the kitchen, stroking Sharon's head, as she passed. She'd picked up a bottle of brandy, that had been displayed in a china cabinet in the living room and she went through the kitchen cabinets and found three glasses.

Amanda poured three large brandies and sat down beside the others. Sharon was shaking so much when she took her first sip, that brandy was spilling out over the rim of the glass, but after couple of sips she settled.

Cynthia stood up and started going through the Kitchen cupboards, 'fucking hell, he's made this a home from home. There's every kind of chocolate bar, pop, hot dogs, all the stuff kids like.' Amanda looked up, 'well if you were a sixteen-year-old, who'd stood and watched as your mother spent all her money on cigarettes and cider and nothing for you and your sister all your childhood, wouldn't you grab every treat you could if it was suddenly free?'

Sharon held out her glass, 'pour me another, will you. Can I lie down somewhere?' Cynthia stood up, 'I'll check upstairs, you stay here with Amanda. I'll find something to replace the top you lost.'

Cynthia walked up the stairs. There were four doors. The first one she tapped on then opened, was a bathroom. There was no sound coming from any of the rooms, but she knocked on each door, just in case. When she was sure it was safe, she entered the first bedroom.

The room was tidy, with a single bed and a wardrobe and drawers, a typical teenager's room. She went through the drawers and found a light grey hoody that looked like it would fit Sharon. She called down the stairs and Amanda came to the bottom stair. Cynthia tossed the hoody down to Amanda and Amanda went back into the kitchen.

Cynthia checked the next, a double room. Again, the bed was made and the room was tidy. It was the main bedroom and there was a dressing table, fitted wardrobes, two sets of drawers and a king-sized bed. The double window overlooked Millfield.

There were lots of clothing in the wardrobes and Cynthia undressed out of her dirty clothing and pulled on clean leggings, a tee shirt and thick, baggy navy jumper.

Cynthia entered the last room. It was obvious right away that this was the room Alec Donaldson had been using. It also overlooked Millfield.

Cynthia looked out. The four dead were now at the far side of the field and it was quiet out front. She turned and looked around the room.

There was a single bed, that was untidily made. There was a wardrobe and a long chest of drawers with cans of beer, sweets and piles of money, strewn across the top. There were stacks of food from floor to ceiling and a pile of boxes of crisps along the window wall.

Ominously, on top of the crisp boxes there were a number of hunting knives, all of them having been badly cleaned, leaving behind residue of blood.

There were also four lengths of rope, you know, the sort used for clothes lines, each cut to a couple of feet in length.

In front of the bed was a video camera on a tripod, pointed over the bed. Cynthia walked over to the bed and switched on the camera and rewound the tape. There was a 'play' option and she pressed it and bent over and watched the small screen.

The footage started with a tied up and gagged semi - naked girl lying on the bed, crying and terrified. Alec Donaldson spoke from behind the camera, 'you do everything I say, now or your fucking dead, do you understand?' The terrified girl nodded. She looked about fourteen years old. Her feet were tied to either side of the bed and she was only covered by a pair of pink panties and a vest top.

As the footage continued, Alec Donaldson came into shot completely naked, with a hunting knife in his hand. As he used the knife to cut the girl's panties free, Cynthia pressed 'pause.'

Cynthia stepped back, horrified. She glanced to the side at the knives. The knife Alec had in his hand in the clip, was on top of the boxes, 'Jesus Christ.' Cynthia looked back at the camera. There was a mesh bag attached to the tripod and she put her hand in the bag. There were more tapes. She ejected the current tape and inserted one of the others.

When she pressed play it was similar. A different girl tied to the bed, semi naked, Alec entering the scene, cutting off what remained of her clothing.

Cynthia pressed fast forward and looked away from the rape scene. When she glanced back at the screen, Cynthia quickly pressed play. The screen was dark, but she could make out the camera was focusing on the field outside.

The footage zoomed in and out until there was a clear picture of the girl in the film. She had been dressed and was wearing leggings, white trainers and a yellow puffer jacket, zipped up.

The girl appeared still, lying on her side, but as the image zoomed in her fingers were moving.

In a few minutes, Cynthia realised what was happening. Alec Donaldson had killed the girl and was filming her reanimating outside. She watched as the girl got to her feet, stood for a while, then clumsily walked off, tripping and falling numerous times.

Cynthia pressed fast forward and stepped away, in horror, but the horror was nothing compared to what she saw, as she returned to switch off the camera. She'd pressed pause, just as her husband, Sammy Dodds had entered the frame. He was sat on the bed beside a dark-haired girl, around fifteen years old, who was fully naked and tied to the bed.

She pressed play and Sammy Dodds was talking to the girl, 'I promise you'll not be hurt if you're good, Lec, fuck off out the room now, you don't harm the girl, after, right?' 'Aye, I promise, if she does what you say,' 'and Lec, that fucking camera better not be on. I'll shout on you when I'm done.' Cynthia could hear the door open and close as Alec left the room and she watched as Sammy undressed and knelt between the legs of the child he was about to rape. Cynthia wanted to press 'stop,' but was frozen, as her husband had his way with the terrified girl.

When it was over, Sammy Dodds could just be seen dressing in the corner of the shot. The girl lay silent, in a state of terror. Sammy then called for Alec, who came into the room, as Sammy left. Alec could be seen stood over the bed, watching out the window for Sammy to go. Cynthia pressed stop as Alec Donaldson knelt down on the bed, over the girl and commenced strangling her.

Cynthia tried to call for Amanda but no sound came out of her mouth. She swallowed hard and called again, then turned and vomited against the wall radiator, under the window.

Amanda entered the room. Cynthia pressed play and walked out. She was white as a sheet, unable to say anything.

Amanda Blewitt realised, as she fast forwarded through the rest of the tapes, that her husband, Gary, Craig Thompson, Abe Gardener and Sammy Dodds had been raping young girls, that Alec Donaldson had stalked and captured. None of the Donaldson brothers appeared, just Gary, Abe, Craig and Sammy. There was no way Alec would have let his father and uncles in on his business.

Dad would have just taken over and uncles Jimmy and Mick would never have given him a turn at the girls, like the others did.

Amanda spent a half hour fast forwarding through the tapes, then turned off the camera and went downstairs.

As Amanda was pouring a brandy, Cynthia put her arm around her, 'was any of the other men involved, Amanda?' 'No, no, just Sammy, I'm, I'm sorry Cynthia.'

Amanda had taken the two tapes showing Gary, Craig and Abe, raping They were in the zipped part of a handbag, she'd acquired from the main bedroom. Amanda had decided she would destroy them when she got the chance. She was now commencing a process of denial.

Amanda passed drinks to the others, 'he had footage of Jimmy and Mick fucking Kylie in their sitting room. He must have been filming them before all this started. The footage had been taken from outside, through the window.

Alec was always looking through windows. On the tape, Mick was fucking her from behind, while she was sucking Jimmy's cock. She must have been fucking the two of them when Ray was at work, fucking drunken whore, swallowing a load of cum and washing it down with neat vodka, while being pounded by another bloke, nasty.'

Cynthia took a drink, 'God Almighty, if Ray had found that camera?'

Amanda continued, 'It wasn't just a one off. The same tape had a few occasions. She was giving them both a hand job on one, while Jimmy was feeding her vodka from a bottle, absolutely vile.' Cynthia started to cry, 'I can't believe Sammy...' Amanda took a drink of brandy, 'nothing we can do now. He's gone, Cyn. We have to get past this and survive.'

The following morning, Sharon looked out of the main bedroom window. The three had all slept in the large bed and were getting dressed, 'something's going on out there.' They all stood back from the window, overlooking the field.

There were men at the Donaldson house and the huge stores of food and drink, the Donaldsons had amassed, were being taken away.

One of the men was constructing a large pile of pallets and had a pattern laid out on the grass that appeared like the shape of a room inside and the pile was being built around it. As the day progressed the heap of wood was in the region of twenty feet high. Occasionally dead had approached the men, but they were killed quickly and efficiently and just dropped against the pile.

The three women had plenty food and hadn't needed to venture out, but Amanda had seen one of the men look over a number of times. She told the others she thought they had been spotted.

The three women sat in the kitchen by candlelight, that night. Cynthia's mood had dramatically changed and she was in a deep low mood.

Sharon was coming to terms with what had happened and now communicating better.

Amanda was putting on a brave face. She wanted no one to know Gary had been involved in what had gone on in this house. She looked at the others, 'we need to get out of here. I think the Hollymount lot know someone's here. When they're finished what they are doing over there, they'll be over, Sharon, what do you think?' 'I think the bastard who killed Craig needs to pay for what he's done. Kylie and Alec would have made their way to her brother, Ken. He lives in New Hartley, Maple Court. If he's survived, he'd take us in.'

Cynthia looked up, 'how are we going to get there? Everyone knows the Horton Road, Spine Road and all the way down to New Hartley and Deleval is overrun. There's no way past.'

Amanda stood up and cleared the chocolate bar wrappers and empty beer cans into the bin, 'Our best option is to hole out here and hope I'm wrong about being seen, but if we get a chance in the next couple of days we need to move. We can carry supplies; I saw knapsacks in one of the rooms.

Maybe we could move up to the other end of Bedlington, somewhere, like North Ridge or Redhouse Farm. Find an empty house and stay put. We might even find survivors that will take us in.'

Cynthia looked over her shoulder, as she made for the living room, 'aye, take us in and what? What do you think men will do with three widowed women when there's no law? If we go out there, we're done for, in more ways than one. If I'm going to die in the next few days, I'd rather go at the end of Don Mason's gun than have my throat cut after a gang rape. I'm staying put. We've got supplies. If they come, they come.'

There was more activity on the field from early the next morning and the last of the supplies were being taken from the house.

The three women stayed upstairs all day, occasionally looking out, but there was a lot of activity late afternoon.

Amanda was stood at the window, 'they've got Alec, that Ian Clarke is leading him into the wood pile. There's blood all over Alec's head.' She continued watching for a few minutes, 'they're bringing Ray, in a wheelchair, Jesus, he looks in a bad way. He's being bundled into the wood pile as well and there's two gone in with him.'

Amanda continued to watch, 'They've come back out. Everyone's gone inside Ray's house. They've just left Ray and Alec. What the fuck are they doing?'

Nothing was happening, so Amanda sat back on the bed with the others and they chatted over a few cans of Alec's lager.

A bit later Amanda ran to the window. There were loud screams coming from the field. She looked over, but it was very dark and hard to focus, 'I think it's Ray, they're doing something to Ray. She could just make out the movement of people surrounding the pile, then she saw a flame.

As the fire got stronger and lit up the field, Amanda saw the group of people leaving Millfield, towards the Front Street. The screaming continued for a few more minutes, then stopped.

A short time later, thousands of Dead entered Millfield from all directions. They gathered around the fire, transfixed. Millfield was like a packed football stadium, as the dead took up all available space. The three could see the crowd going back as far as and onto the front street. The fire had attracted almost every zombie in Bedlington, so the women just got comfortable, to wait it out.

Sharon was asleep on the bed and Amanda was laid down on her back, beside her, 'we've got no chance to get out, now, Cynthia. Looks like we are staying put, but I don't think Don Mason will bother us with this lot here. They seem content to just stand and watch the fire. If we keep quiet, they'll not be interested in the house. Home sweet home.'
Amanda got up off the bed, 'Come on Cyn.' The two of them went downstairs. Amanda opened a kitchen cabinet, 'yes, I thought I saw this earlier.' She reached up and pulled out a litre bottle of Bacardi, 'grab a few cans of Pepsi, Cyn, let's all get smashed.'

The following day, the dead were still congregated on the field. It was like the only stimuli around, was the burnt down fire, still smoldering and smoking. Some had sat on the ground, but most were looking around, heads on their sides, listening, smelling for anything they could feed on. They had been there all night, so they were, no doubt hungry and at their most dangerous.

The three women sat silent all day, never leaving the bedroom.

It was dark outside when they heard the sound of mass footsteps. There was so many dead walking, the ground was pounding, vibrating through the house. They were all making for the Twenty Acres Field, past their hideout, 'listen,' Amanda was at the window. In the distance there was the sound of continual pops and she carefully opened the window, put her head out and looked out over the field. There was a massive display of fireworks going off in the distance. The dead were heading off towards the sound and lights in the sky.

Amanda carefully closed the window. 'Someone's setting fireworks off up past the golf course, drawing them away from here. They're all leaving.'

It was a few minutes before five o'clock, the following morning when Don Mason tapped his spike on the front door. Cynthia got up and went to the window, 'It's him, Don Mason. You were right. They know we're here.'

Amanda got out of bed and opened the window, 'what do you want, Mason? We barely just made it here. You need to give us time to move. There were thousands of dead here last night. I know Clarke had seen us at the window. All we ask is time and we'll go. God Almighty, what's that smell, what?'

Don looked up to the window, 'call it a repellant, look. after all that's gone on, enough is enough. Ray and Alec Donaldson died in that fire. They were the threat to us and all survivors in Bedlington and I know you lost your men, but we had to defend our homes. Stay here. We have no fight with you three, now, as long as you aren't a threat to us. You won't be harmed if we come across you looking for food. None of us want any more death.'

Amanda nodded and Don turned and walked back towards the front street.

2

Seeking Survivors

After the dead had lay down, Don Mason (Mace), Mark Mijeson (Midgy), Ian Clarke (Clarky) and Davy Dawson (Dowser), were in Don's kitchen, discussing the next rescue venture.

Midgy, put his hand in the box and pulled out a piece of paper. As he opened it up, Don held out his hand and Midgy passed it to him.

Don took the remaining sheets of folded paper out of the box and put them in his pocket, 'the dead were running out of energy, lying down, yesterday and I expect more so today. We need to take this opportunity and get out to all the remaining houses. Let's do it in one fair swoop.'

Vic Hind and Connor Castle, the two men Don had met on the Horton Road, entered the kitchen, along with Ronnie Binns, resident of the Square. Dowser's son, Paul came in behind them, with Hannah Rice. Hannah sat on the kitchen bench, 'Geordie is coming over from the farm. Heather's parents' names are still in the box.'

Don took the sheets of paper back out of his pocket, 'that's fine, Hannah. Who wants to start?'

Vic stepped forward, 'Aren't we missing an opportunity, here? the dead have run out of food. They're lying down. I was out earlier. Hardly any are on their feet. I say we spend the rest of this week finishing them. Spike them, load them on a trailer, dig a massive hole and bury them somewhere in a mass grave. There're bulldozers all over, where works were abandoned.' Geordie had just entered, 'There's one by the farm. We've already used it for reinforcing the walls.'

Midgy spoke up, 'There are still a few addresses. It will only take a day to get around them. With the amount of people here, we could make up two groups, each taking half. We don't want to miss the chance we've been given. Just one day to check on our people's families then we'll get out and clear up the mess. Geordie, you've still got family out there?'

Geordie nodded, 'I'm with Midgy. Get our people first. What about all of the new arrivals? Paul, has Marie got family out there?' Paul nodded, 'we all have someone. I want to check on Marie's folks, I'm with Midgy, as well.'

Don laid the sheets of paper on the table, 'Hannah, Colleen's parents live up Hazelmere. That's beside Meadowdale school isn't it?' 'Aye, if you pull out Featherstone Grove - that's down the bottom of the new estate. The address at North Ridge is on route. I know all these places.'

Don handed three addresses to Hannah and looked at the ones left, 'Bower Grange, Waverly Avenue and the Oval.' Midgy took the sheets, I know the area. We used to play footer on the Oval playing field. It's an NHS building now. We could head down Rothsay Terrace, do Striling Drive, back out through Waverly and follow the back streets to the Oval. I'll take a group.' After further conversation it was decided that Hannah would lead group one, consisting of herself, Don, Vic, Dowser and Paul. Midgy would lead the group, consisting of Himself, Geordie, Ronnie, Clarky and Vic.

Don addressed all the friends, 'please be careful out there. We don't know for sure the dead are finished, so keep a wide berth. Get some weapons and we'll all leave around nine o'clock and remember, it's highly likely we'll be delivering bad news on our return so any survivor is a blessing, here.' He took the Browning twenty - two calibre and checked it was fully loaded.

Don knelt beside Jamie, 'I'm going out seeking survivors. If you need company, pop along to Dawn's, Vic will be out as well, maybe you could watch a film or something?' Jamie looked up and smiled, 'I'm ok, grandad, I've got stuff to do today, thanks.'

At nine o'clock, the two groups entered the Front Street from the main gate. They made their way up the main road, passing dozens of dead bodies, most laid on their backs, mouths open and eyes closed. Hannah poked one with the spiked rounders bat Don had made her, 'this is weird, look at them all. It's like they've all taken a final resting position.' Don looked around, 'Jesus, I've never seen anything like this. Crows and gulls as far as the eye can see. They must have sensed easy pickings.'

Crows were making a lot of noise and they were out in force. Every building in sight had crows perched on the ridge tiles, watching down.

Seagulls were also congregating in numbers, awkwardly trying to maintain a roost on the sloping roofs, while not brave enough to challenge the crows for the better position. There were a lot of birds overhead and the lamp posts and trees were quickly becoming occupied. The sky was dark with birds gliding around in vast numbers.

The groups separated at the Northumberland Arms and Hanna's group watched on as Midgy led the others down past what was once the 'Monkey' pub and into Beech Grove.

* * *

As Hannah's group approached the Red Lion roundabout, she stopped and looked around, 'look at all these crows. I've seen nothing like it, Don,' 'not just crows, Hannah, jackdaws, rooks, magpies and a few types of sea bird, as well. Looks like they're assembling for a free meal,' 'free meal? It's like something from Hitchcock. There're thousands of them, as far as you can see in all directions.'

Don knelt down beside one of the dead, just as it closed its mouth on a few flies. He called out, 'keep your distance from these things, as long as there's still life in them, they can still bite. Consider them dangerous. Once the birds get brave enough, the feeding will start and that should hopefully finish them. We'll make our way straight along Ridge Terrace to the school entrance.'

The road along Ridge Terrace was blocked both sides by abandoned cars and the paths strewn with dead bodies, most laid on their backs, hands under their chins and some, laid out with head wounds. The stench of rotting bodies was hardly bearable, as the group headed along past West End First School, then on towards the CO OP store, that was previously the Ridge Farm pub and carvery.

Dowser and Paul crossed the road from the CO OP and made their way into Hazelmere Avenue, a line of two storey flats, that led along towards Meadowdale middle school. Paul turned and waved at the others, 'clear path in here, come on.'

Hannah, Don and Connor crossed the road and the group made their way down Hazelmere Avenue.

'That's the one.' Hannah made her way to a front door and banged hard on the brass knocker. There was no response. Dowser stepped forward and took a crowbar from his knapsack, 'here, I'll prise the door, Don, you be ready there.'

Don stood ready with the spike.

The latch popped, the door swung open and Don carefully stepped inside. There was a woman on the floor, on her back, just like the dead outside. Hannah stepped into the doorway, 'It's Amy, Don.'

Don took the spike and pierced Amy Rice through the temple.'

Hannah called out, 'Bob, are you in here?' There was silence for a few moments, then they heard movement in the kitchen. Don and Hannah stepped back as the door was bumped against and they heard the sound of something being scraped against the floor, then the door opened, 'Hannah, is that you?' Hannah stepped forward and hugged Bob in the doorway, as he entered the room.

He looked down at the floor, 'Amy, Amy,' 'I know, Bob, she was gone, when we got here. She's at rest now. Bob, have you been bitten?' 'no.' Bob stood, arms folded, nervously looking around. He was in his early sixties, white haired and thin, wearing dark trousers, slippers and a dark green Marks and Spencer's pullover. Hannah's first impression was that Bob looked about fifteen years older that the last time she'd seen him.

Dowser and Paul took Amy's body and carried her outside. Bob sat down on the settee, 'I've been in the kitchen for a week, Hannah. I told Amy not to go outside in all the commotion, but she saw someone running from the dead, a young girl, she was cornered. She only opened the door to give her a place to run to, but one of them was outside and grabbed Amy's arm. I pulled her back inside and got the door closed, but she'd been bitten. I managed to stop the bleeding and dress the wound, but she took a turn for the worst and… she was alive and sleeping most of the day, the shock, you know? I must have dozed off.

When I woke up Amy was trying to get to her feet. I knew straight away she'd died and what she'd become, we've seen them outside. I made for the kitchen and put a chair against the door. I've been there since. A couple of days ago she stopped pushing against the door.'

Connor entered the sitting room, 'look, Mr Rice, Bob, we're here to take you back to Hollymount Square. Your daughter's there, but we're going to the bottom of Alnwick Drive, along the road, there and back up to North Ridge. We don't want to leave you here, so do you think you'll manage the walk?' 'yes, son, I'll manage, Hannah, Colleen. She's alright?' 'Not just alright, Bob, but you've got a baby granddaughter waiting to meet you.' Stay close to me and we'll get you back. I'm sorry, but we have to leave Amy here. Do you need to grab a few things? We'll not be back.'

Bob nodded, went into the bedroom and collected his watch and Amy's jewellery box. Hannah opened her knapsack, 'here, Bob, I'll carry them for you. Lets' catch the others up.'

Bob glanced at his wife's body, as he exited through the front door, 'I'm sorry, Amy, I'm so sorry I have to leave you.' Hannah put her arm around him and they left for the next address.

* * *

Ronnie Binns pushed a body over, as the group were entering Beech Grove, 'It's Colin Markem.' Midgy stepped forward and looked down at the body. The broken arm Colin had sustained when he'd betrayed the residents of the square was at ninety degrees, almost black with internal bleeding. There was a puncture hole through Colin's head. Midgy stepped away, 'looks like the cunt didn't get far. Serves the fucker right. We'd have been Donaldson's slaves, if he'd succeeded, or worse.'

They made their way down Beech Grove, past Hirst Villas and took a left onto the long straight road of Rothsay Terrace, passing dozens of abandoned and crashed cars. There were significantly less dead on this road, but there were still crows and carrion birds on top of all houses, lamp posts and trees.

Ronnie looked skyward, 'this is fucking creeping me out, all these birds. What the fuck is going on?' Vic walked across and patted Ronnie on the back, 'They hold court, you know, crows do. If one of them is being an arsehole, upsetting the harmony and causing distress, the court will sit and they make a decision, sentence, if you like.

Quite often a crow court will lead to an execution and the culprit will be chased down and pecked to death. Maybe the crows have seen enough killing. Maybe they've decided enough is enough and it's on them to put a stop to it.' He smiled at Ronnie, 'or maybe they're just seeing the buffet opening.'

Ronnie was still troubled. He looked around again, then at Vic, 'well I've always thought a gathering of crows signified death, a sign of impending evil, even.' Vic patted him on the back, 'well there's plenty death around, Ronnie, son, plenty death and I would say that, when death can walk around, evil isn't that far away, either.'

There were bodies laid out all the way down Rothsay Terrace, but no signs of life and no signs of any dead on their feet. Only the birds cawing broke the silence and it was very loud.

After about half a mile the group approached a Spar garage and store.

The doors were jammed open and the shelves empty. There was zombie slime and blood everywhere, inside and the group slipped past and into Bower Grange estate.

Midgy led the way, 'If we follow the main road in past Harewood and Woburn, there's an entrance on the left. He took the sheet of paper, 'Eight Striling Drive, Chris Dewhirst, come on.'

The group reached the entrance to Harewood and Woburn Drive. There were a lot of bodies with head injuries. All had been laid on their backs, like all the dead en route, but someone had finished them. Midgy gathered the group together, 'there's a high likelihood there's living down here…shit! Keep calm everybody.'

There were four groups of three men surrounding them, all armed with knives, and makeshift clubs, mostly hardwood table legs and baseball bats. They had seen the group coming and hid behind abandoned cars.

One of the men stepped forward, 'nothing here for you guys, now, leave those bags, turn around and go.' He was a young man in his thirties, black gelled back hair and he was wearing dark jeans, a combat jacket and Doc Martin boots. Midgy looked around the men. They looked quite well dressed, probably survivors from the estate, that had stayed together, scavenging for what they need.

Midgy stepped forward, 'we want no trouble. We're looking for a man, that's all. We just want to check on his house in Stirling Drive, then we'll be away.' The leader of the group nodded and three men with knives approached the group.

As the group stepped back, Vic walked towards the attackers. Clarky was scrambling to get the revolver out of the bag and called Vic back, 'what the fuck are you doing, Vic?' but it was too late. As the three men went for Vic, he sidestepped a lunging knife, twisted the arm and took the knife out of the attacker's hand, putting him to the ground, in the same motion. Vic then kicked him in the side, immobilising him, as the second man attacked.

Vic sidestepped again taking the attacker by the arm and making three punches to the throat. The attacker dropped, as Vic stepped into the third attack, disarmed the attacker, putting his arm up his back and held his own knife to his throat.

Vic looked over at the leader of the group, 'right, I'm going to let this mug go and you lot will fuck off. The next person that attacks me or any of this group will die, then I will kill you all, do I make myself clear?'

Vic pushed the attacker away and he ran over to his friends. The other two crawled in the same direction and were helped to their feet.

The leader stepped forward, 'my name's Dean Cane. We're survivors just like you. Who are you looking for?' Clarky dropped the revolver back into the bag, 'Margaret Hipsburn asked us to look for her brother Chris Dewhirst. We've secured our homes and we're looking for family members. The address we have is Stirling Drive.'

It was silent for a few moments and a man stepped out of the group, 'I'm Chris Dewhirst.' Chris was tall and stocky, around forty years old. He had long dark brown hair and a beard and he was wearing jeans, Timberland boots and a thick navy hoodie.

Chris looked at Dean Cane and Dean nodded, 'looks like Chris is moving on.' He put an arm around Chris, 'all the best, friend. I hope your sis and Neil are ok' The gang turned and walked off into Woburn Drive.

Midgy walked over to Chris and shook hands with him. 'Chris, my name is Midgy, this is Geordie, Ronnie, Clarky and this fucker here is Bruce Lee, also known as Vic. Do you need to collect anything from home?' 'no, I haven't been back there, my girlfriend…' He swallowed hard, but couldn't continue, 'no, lets' just go.'

As they made their way back towards Station Road, Clarky stepped alongside Vic and whispered in his ear, 'we need to talk.' Vic turned and looked him in the eye, 'I know.'

Midgy led the group towards Station Road, 'Cross over here, the entrance to Waverly is just along the road.'

* * *

Hannah's group reached the roundabout that led into Alnwick Drive and Hannah stopped and looked around. The road towards Nedderton was completely blocked by cars and she could see dead bodies laid over bonnets and face down on the ground, 'looks like there was a real fight here. A lot of these bodies have gunshot wounds.' Don walked over to one of the bodies, 'shotgun, by the looks of it. It's all farmland around Nedderton. I wonder if they were trying to clear the place.
Will's house is along the road, down a small lane. I think I know the one, but he was using the fields to get around. He came back for the elderly residents the kids were looking after.

Maybe it wasn't just the kids looking after the old folks. I reckon a group with shotguns have worked from the field, over there, look at the mass of bodies along the hedgerow. Looks like they made their way along, adjacent to the road, shooting all the zombies.

Look, about fifty yards along there are cars blocking the way right up to the hedges, just like on the Horton Road. Bodies are piled up over there. I'd bet they've done that on the Stannington side, as well.'

Nedderton was a small village, just outside Bedlington, with a main road running through the centre. There weren't many houses, but the central main road made the whole place vulnerable. It was obvious a huge effort had gone into blocking the ways in and out.

Hannah stood beside Don and looked along the road, 'we should ask Will about this when we return. If there are survivors at the farm, we may be able to work together, clearing bodies and cars.'

Hanna made her way across the road onto Alnwick Drive and the group followed. There were dead on the ground all the way down towards Featherston, most laid on their backs and the crows and carrion birds, were perched at every available vantage point.

Magpies had flown down to the ground and were walking towards bodies and walking away, as if teasing them for a reaction, but the dead laid still. It was a long road down to Featherstone Grove. As they neared, Paul and Dowser ran on ahead. There were no signs of survivors, anywhere, all the way down Alnwick Drive.

The others in the group stopped to give Bob a rest and Hannah passed him a bottle of water, 'don't worry, Bob, the last stop is on the way back, then we head home. It's safe where we're going.' 'I'm alright, Hannah, I do a lot of walking, just not lately. I'll not slow you down.'

Dowser was stood outside Kevin and Sarah Hughes' house, with an arm around Paul, as the group caught them up. Paul was head in hands, crying. Dowser looked at Don and shook his head.

Don walked across and put his hand on Paul's shoulder, 'I'm sorry son.' Paul looked up, 'how am I going to tell Marie?'

Don looked around the group. Everyone had their heads down. He walked into the house. Kevin Hughes was laid on his back, hands on his chest, under his chin. He had two bites, one to his forearm and another to his shoulder. His wife was laid on the settee. She had bites to her neck and face and her lower body had been eaten, leaving a cavity that exposed her spine, 'Jesus, he's turned and eaten his own wife.' Don put the spike through the heads of the two bodies and left the house.

The birds were noisy, as the group made their way back along Alnwick Drive, as if the Crows and seagulls disapproved of the Magpies being first to inspect the bodies, but had still opted to stay a safe distance away, themselves.

As the group reached the roundabout, Hannah pointed across the road, towards North Ridge and called out, 'I think Meadowdale Crescent is one of the streets across there.'

They crossed the road and saw the sign for Meadowdale Crescent. Don sat down on a brick garden wall and took a drink. He passed the drink to Dowser, 'listen, we'll take it from here. Take Paul and Bob back to the Square. You've been through enough. If Hector Fisher is here, we'll not be far behind you.'

Paul was white as a sheet and shaking. Dowser glanced at him and passed the drink back to Don, 'aye, I think your right, Don. We'll head back. Be careful in there, mind.'

Don held his hand out to Paul and gave him Marie's parents' wedding rings, he'd removed before leaving them, 'I thought Marie would...' 'thanks, Don, thanks. I wouldn't have thought.'

As Dowser left with Paul and Bob, Hannah, Don and Connor entered Meadowdale Crescent.

* * *

Midgy's group made their way down Waverly Drive. They saw dead walking for the first time, two men, faces covered in blood. One was carrying what was left of a small black dog.

The two dead glanced at the group and continued walking aimlessly along the road. Geordie walked across to them and one at a time took them down with his baseball bat. He made his way back to the group, 'they just stand there and look at you when their stomachs are full. Don't even put their hands up to protect themselves.' Clarky nodded, 'aye, the only instinct the fuckers seem to have held on to, is the need to eat. Nothing else.'

Midgy stopped outside a house half way along Waverly Drive, 'it's this one. Young Julie's dad lives here, Ted Knight.'

The bedroom window opened and a man called down to them, 'what do you want? I have nothing of value and very little food.' Midgy looked up, 'are you Ted Knight? Julie Knight sent us. She's safe and our place is secure. We've come to take you there. You need to come now. There is still some dead walking around, but we have a safe route home.'

Ted Knight stood silent for a few moments. He was fifty-five years old, medium height with overgrown, dark hair, that was so greasy it looked wet. He was wearing a dark sweater, with food stains down the front and he was unshaven. He walked back from the window and in a few moments the front door opened, 'I'm sorry, my appearance, I…'

Clarky smiled and shook his hand, we've all been there, mate, we'll do you a bath, get you fresh clothes and the lasses will even cut your hair. When was the last time you had a hot meal? They bake, your daughter and her friends, you know. Howay, Ted, pick up anything you need to bring and come with us.'

Ted walked out and closed the door behind him. His cotton tracksuit bottoms, once light grey were dark and grubby and he was wearing plaid slippers, you know, the ones dads always get for Christmas, 'I've got nowt, marra, nowt that's any use these days.'

The group made their way along Waverley Drive, towards Roslin Park. Clarky walked with Ted, 'tell me, Ted, how have you survived so long?' 'by staying indoors, mate. It was carnage out there, the first few days, when the dead showed up.

People seemed to be drawn to them, either trying to help them, or fighting with them, when they realised, they were dangerous.
I survived by leaving them alone. Staying out of their way. I've only ever gone out when I run out of food, but not far.

I've survived from the cupboards of the neighbour's houses. A lot of the dead, lying around here, are my neighbours. Sid, over there, was my best mate. He came here when he'd been bitten.'

Clarky looked across the road. There was a grey-haired man, with a thick moustache, lying on his back, just like all the other dead in the street. His body appeared covered in bites, face, neck, arms, legs, bites all over. Ted continued, 'begged me to let him in, he did, but I knew by then, the bites make you turn. He got dragged away by the others.

Funny how violent they can be towards a living man, but when he was dead, they just lost interest in him.

When he turned, he was one of them. Walking around with the people who killed him, as if all is forgiven. After begging me for help, he'd take a chunk out of me now, given half a chance.

They have no friends or family when they turn, mate, you're just food to them.'

The group reached Roslin Park and stopped for a rest and a drink. Midgy took the last sheet of paper, 'the house is on the corner, just opposite Foundry House. The Oval leads out to Stead Lane and back up towards home. All being well, we should be well on our way before lunchtime.'

They all had a drink of water, then made their way along Roslin Park.

* * *

Meadowdale Crescent was a collection of terraced houses, just off North Ridge, that ran in a semi - circle, with an entrance / exit, either side. Both entrances had been blocked by cars and someone had taken time to plug gaps with bags of rubble.

Hannah, Don and Connor climbed over the barrier and entered the Crescent. A few garden walls had been knocked down, accounting for the rubble, but the front gardens were all tidy, grass and hedges cut and weed free.

Hector Fisher's house was mid - way along the Crescent, on the side that overlooks the main road and they made their way to the front door.

Don knocked on the door and it swung open. He entered the house; spike raised and made his way to the living room. Hannah stood watch outside and Connor entered and headed upstairs.

The downstairs was empty. Don was going through the kitchen cupboards when Connor came back downstairs, 'nothing up there, Don. He must have left' 'There's nothing in the cupboards, Connor. The place has been cleared. There're people here, just not this house.'

The two men went back outside and looked around. Don looked up at the rooftops, 'no birds here, no bodies anywhere. This place has been cleared and maintained. This is somebody's home.' He walked into the middle of the road and called out, 'My name is Don Mason. I'm looking for Hector Fisher, or any survivors. Jim Fisher asked me to call on Hector.'

They stood silent for a few moments, then heard a voice. 'Hector is dead. I have a graveyard in one of the gardens. His grave is marked. I'm sorry for your loss.'

A young man was standing in one of the front gardens a few yards from Hannah, Don and Connor. He was tall and well built, with long, tied back, long, thick black hair and dressed in black jeans, black Nirvana tee shirt and a grey, washed out denim jacket.

The young man let his hair down, as Don approached the garden. He had been weeding and there was a hoe stuck in the ground alongside a plastic bucket full of weeds.

The man stood, head down, appearing uncomfortable in demeanour and spoke, 'Everyone left, but for a few and they didn't last long.

I'm the only survivor here. Some locked themselves in their houses, but when they ran out of food, they made for other houses. That's what happened to Hector Fisher. He was bitten and turned.

I suffer anxiety and depression and struggle among people. I just completely withdrew. I couldn't go out there, but I had to in the end, when the food ran out. I put Hector and a lot of dead down, all in one morning. Then I blocked the entrances.

When I was sure it was safe, I buried them all. I turned one of the gardens into a graveyard. I marked the graves of the people I knew. The others are in a mass grave, twenty of them, men women…kids.' A tear was making its way down the man's cheek, 'my name is Mark Fitzgerald. I'm sorry, but I'm the only one here.'

Connor stepped forward, 'Mark, what about the road along the way at Nedderton. It's all blockaded there. Are there survivors?' 'I think so. There was a day when there was a lot of gunfire. That's the day when I went outside. The dead had left, attracted to the noise.

I blocked the way with cars and filled some bags with bricks and anything heavy I could find. The shooting went on all day. In the afternoon I went door to door with a crowbar. The neighbours who had been bitten and got back inside, including Hector had turned. I…I prised each door and ended them with the crowbar.'

Don stepped inside and made to put his hand on Mark's shoulder, 'that's ok, Mark,' 'please…' Mark stepped back, away from the contact, 'please, I can't, I don't…' Don stepped back and held up his hand, 'it's ok, son, I understand. We have a safe place, Hollymount square. There's room for you there. We have plenty gardens,' 'no, I'm better alone, Don. Please don't make me come with you. I have all the gardens planted up. I'm ok here. I just need to be on my own.'

Don looked at Hannah and Connor and nodded, 'I'll ask our survivors not to include this area, when they are seeking supplies, but if you need anything, don't hesitate to come to Hollymount Square and, don't forget, Mark, the living are dangerous, as well, now.'

Mark took the hoe and watched as Hannah, Don and Connor climbed the barrier and left.

* * *

Midgy's group were outside Heather Wells' parents' home, when the shot rang out. Ronnie Binns spun round and fell over the garden wall. The group ducked behind cars, as the second shot was fired. Thousands of birds had taken flight and the noise was deafening.

Vic crawled through the garden gate and over to Ronnie, 'let me see that.' Ronnie was breathing heavy and wincing with pain, 'fuck, shit, I've been fucking shot!' Vic pulled back Ronnie's shirt, revealing a really deep gash across his shoulder, which was bleeding quite heavily. He took his bag off his shoulder and took out a tea towel, 'hold that tight on there, Ronnie. I know it hurts, but you're going to be ok. Clarky, can you reach a car mirror?'

Clarky and the others were sat against a car, hoping they were out of sight of the shooter. Clarky grabbed the car wing mirror, just above his head, pulled it off and threw it over the wall. Vic lifted the mirror with his right hand, then lifted his bag above the wall with his left. Another shot rang out and the bag flew across the garden.

Vic was lying on his back, 'the shooter is in an upstairs window, up past the shops, over there. He's firing a high calibre rifle. Clarky, I'm going to need that handgun.' Clarky took the pistol out of the bag, made sure the safety was on and threw it over the wall.

Vic lifted the mirror so he could see Clarky, 'listen, we need a distraction. Can you crawl along and set fire to the car at the front?'

Clarky took a crowbar and some matches out of his bag, 'can do, Vic, but we'll need to shift.' 'I know, don't ignite the petrol tank. Wrap a rag around the crowbar and dip it into the petrol tank. Put it under the front wheel and light it. The burning tyre will make enough smoke to give you a chance to get into the house.

Clarky crawled to the front car, and prised off the petrol cap. He took off his checked shirt, tore off the back and wrapped it around the crowbar. After soaking it in the petrol tank, Clarky pushed the rag under the car tyre, struck a match and threw it on. In minutes the car tyre was burning strong and, as it melted, thick black smoke started belching into the air.

Midgy made for the front door and jemmied it open, while Clarky helped Ronnie across the garden and inside. Vic was gone.

When Clarky got inside, Geordie was sat on the settee head in hands. Midgy caught his eye and shook his head. Clarky brushed past him and entered the kitchen. Barny and Tess Martin were lying face down. Both had been shot in the back of the head. They had no bites. Clarky walked back into the sitting room and looked outside. There was still a lot of smoke coming from the fire and he closed the curtains. He sat beside Geordie on the settee and put an arm around him, 'I'm sorry, Geordie.' Geordie nodded.

Midgy had found a first aid kit in a cupboard and was tending to Ronnie's injury, when six shots rang out in the distance, four in quick succession then two more a few seconds apart. Clarky stood up and went to the window, pulling back the curtain, slightly, 'looks like Vic has found them.'

He kept watch and, in a few minutes, Vic was making his way down the middle of the road. He was carrying three handguns, what looked like a Winchester rifle, you know, the ones you see in Cowboy films. Clarky's handgun was tucked in his belt. Vic also had two twenty-two calibre rifles hanging from his left shoulder.

Vic entered the room and passed Clarky his handgun. Clarky took it, but held on to Vic's hand, 'ghost, Vic?' Vic stepped away, 'we'll talk Clarky, let's just get our people back safe.

There were three of them, up there, looked like gun clubbers that have taken up real life hunting. Fucking arseholes. I kneecapped the guy who shot Ronnie. The other two will eat the fucker alive, later.'
Clarky pointed to the kitchen, 'they've been here, Vic.' Vic chose not to look in the kitchen, 'well they'll not be shooting anyone else. Geordie, I'm sorry mate. I wish we'd been able to get here before…'

Geordie stood up, in tears, 'thanks, Vic, thanks to all of you for trying to seek Heather's parents. You could have all been killed, but you did this for us. We both knew it was unlikely they'd be alive, but we've tried. Let's just get ourselves back in one piece. We'll retrieve the bodies, all of them and have a proper funeral when we've cleared the dead.'

Vic passed the Winchester to Ronnie, 'this has to be yours now, Ronnie. If it had hit you full on there'd be a hole right through you. I know it's sore, but count yourself very lucky your still alive. Colleen will stitch it up, when we get back, she's a dab hand. I've got all their ammo in my backpack and mags for the revolvers. They had quite an arsenal.

The group left and made their way past the burning car, along the oval, past Foundry house towards Stead Lane, as thousands of carrion birds were landing back down on their roosts. When the car blew up and the birds all took off again, casting a shadow right across the Oval.

3

A Murder of Crows

The first creatures to arrive when the dead laid down were the flies. They had been swarming anyway, covering bodies that had been permanently put down and the injuries on the longer -dead bodies were infested with maggots.

The dead that had recently gone to ground were all laid out the same. They were on their backs, hands on their chests, laid palms up, just under their chins. Their eyes were closed and mouths open. The only sign they were animated, was the occasional closing and opening of their mouths.

As Don Mason and the group had passed them the day before, no one had noticed this and further inspection would have shown that the flies being trapped in the mouths of the dead was just enough to maintain their awareness. Although too weak to get up and walk around, they had a very small, last reserve of energy, being maintained by the trapping of the flies.

Small birds had been hopping around the bodies, attracted by the maggots that were infesting dead tissue on open wounds and blackbirds, robins and tits were on a non - stop grab and run mission.

Magpies had landed on the ground, first to inspect the dead and they marched towards, then away from the bodies, unable to pluck up the courage to peck at the seemingly easy pickings, the robins and small birds were feasting on.

Eventually, after a lot of cawing, the crows made their move and there was a mass, coordinated take off, from the vantage points, they were holding, down to the ground. Seagulls followed, and there was a lot of confrontation, as they squabbled for access to the bodies. The magpies were quickly flapped away by the crows, but the gulls maintained their stand. Crows and gulls separated, as if in agreement and the ground seemed covered with a shining black carpet, with large patches of light grey and white, where the gulls had established territory.

Gulls and crows gradually braved their way closer to each body, occasionally pecking and flying back to a safe distance, but the dead laid still.

Eventually the birds had made their way onto the bodies, starting to peck at the open wounds.

In an instant, every single dead body opened its eyes. Call it instinct, or a triggered reaction to the presence of the birds, but every dead body on the ground, over the whole of Bedlington opened their eyes, in that very same instant.

The birds' response was to scatter, then quickly return, when the bodies remained still. The eyes were too much of a temptation and, just like the seemingly coordinated opening of the eyes of the dead, the birds saw the eyes as an irresistible prize and, on mass, ran up the bodies.

The noise was deafening, as the dead grabbed birds, that were running over their open hands. Every one of the thousands of birds grabbed, in that moment was bitten and the dead lay, chewing on bird flesh, blood and feathers.

Some birds had escaped the first bite, losing legs, parts of wings, or just suffering deep wounds and they flapped around screaming and panicking, until they flapped onto another body and were grabbed again.

The dead all had one thing in common, insatiable hunger and, within a few minutes of swallowing the flesh of the birds they had grabbed, thousands of dead began sitting up and getting to their feet.

* * *

Dowser, Paul and Bob Rice had made it back to Hollymount Square and were knocking on Colleen's door when the birds screamed. There had been a lot of noise prior, birds in their thousands cawing and jostling for position on the roosts, but this noise was deafening. It brought every resident of the Square outside and people were milling together, confused as to what was happening.

Colleen opened the door and burst into tears, 'dad, oh dad, I'm so pleased you…mam?' Dowser stepped forward and put his hand on her shoulder, 'I'm sorry Colleen, she was gone. It's a miracle your dad has survived. He's been very brave. A real survivor.'

Colleen stood against the door frame, sobbing. Bob took her in his arms, 'come on, Colleen, make me a cup of tea. Hannah told me the two of you have a baby, now? I have to meet her.'

Colleen stepped aside and Bob passed into the house. She looked at Dowser, 'what the living fuck was that noise, Dowser?' Dowser stood head down, 'I think the Dead have just conned every carrion bird in the region. Sounds like they've eaten, so they're about to get back up and our people are out there. I'm going to man the gate, until the others all get back. They'll be in a hurry to get off the street, if the dead get up.'

* * *

Midgy's group were entering Stead Lane, at the junction that once overlooked the Terrier Pub, that had been demolished and developed into supported living bungalows, when the screaming started. They had seen the birds come down, back at the Oval and watched on, as the birds dared to seek the prize of eyeballs, only to be grabbed and bitten.

It was absolute mayhem. Birds were taking off in all directions, the lucky ones that had not been grabbed, went skyward, but there were injured birds flying in all directions around them. They took shelter behind a wall, as a wave of bleeding, injured flapping birds scuttled across the ground, in all directions.

Lots of birds eventually ending up being grabbed by zombies that hadn't yet eaten. There was blood everywhere, as the screaming and scrambling of the birds continued and the volume was significantly increased by the surviving birds, now perched on rooftops, trees and lamp posts, calling out in horror, at what they had just witnessed.

Midgy stood up and looked around.

In all directions, there were zombies, laid on their backs, holding horrifically injured birds to their mouths and, with each bite they took, the volume of injured bird cries reduced, until the only noise was that of the roosting crows and gulls, now walking up and down roofs and along tree branches and lamp posts, in an agitated state. Magpies had flown off earlier, when ousted for position, unaware of their lucky escape.

About a third of the carrion birds, that had crowded, as far as the eye could see had been taken by the dead. They had walked into a perfect trap. The Dead started to sit up, some getting straight to their feet.

Chris Dewhirst scaled the wall, back onto Stead Lane, 'I don't like this. I don't like it at all.' Vic quickly took the guns and gathered the group around, 'who can shoot?' Clarky pulled his revolver. Chris held out his hand, 'I've shot a twenty calibre.' Vic passed him a weapon and poured half a box of rounds into his jacket pocket.

Geordie stepped forward, 'I'll take one, just show me how to load it.' Vic passed a gun to Geordie and quickly demonstrated how to shoot it.

Ronnie was holding the Winchester, and Vic looked over and said, 'Just like the cowboy films, Ronnie, it's fully loaded.'

Midgy took a baseball bat, 'Ted, just stay close. We're going to make a run for home. We can cut across Hudson Avenue, up to Millbank and up Beatty Road. We'll get onto the street just a hundred yards or so from the square.'

Vic held up a hand, 'Listen, the guns are ready to fire, just flick off safety, but remember, only shoot if you have to. The gunshots attract them. Let Midgy hit the odd ones with the bat, rather than firing on them.'

They set off along Stead lane, passing zombies, that were becoming more animated, many reaching out from seated or standing positions, towards them, but the group all kept a safe distance as they ran along Hudson Avenue and onto Millbank Place.

By the time the group reached Beatty Road, the dead were walking. The group reached the bottom of Beatty Road, that joins Millbank Road and all ways were crowded by dead, many on their feet looking around, heads on their sides, listening for any movement.

The group were spotted right away and crowds of dead were making their way towards them from all directions, including behind.

Midgy pointed to the left, 'that way, we can fight our way past and onto the wood head.'

He ran at a group of dead and repeatedly swung the bat, knocking zombies down in his path, but there were too many. Vic and Clarky opened fire, inflicting six headshots and opening a path to the wood head.

Ronnie cocked the Winchester, just as he'd seen in cowboy movies, aimed at a zombie that was approaching Midgy and fired. The shot hit the zombie through the neck but the damage was so severe its head fell to the ground, about ten feet away from the falling body. Ronnie put a hand on where he'd been grazed at the Oval, and gasped as he realised what would have happened to him if the shot had hit him full on.

It was quiet along the overgrown, grassed land, behind Beatty Road and the group made their way to the top of the woods, known as the wood head, where the road leads to Hollymount Avenue.

Some dead had followed them onto the wood head, but were quite a way back. Midgy glanced at Ted, 'you ok?' Ted was out of breath, 'I'll not hold you up. I know what these fuckers can do. You'll not leave me behind, I can guarantee that. Where now?'

Midgy led the way, 'just follow me, Ted, keep close.'

There were several dead on the way along Hollymount Avenue and Midgy flailed the baseball bat at them. Vic supported him, smashing heads with the butt of his rifle and the group eventually made it to the front street adjacent to the Picnic Field bank.

Clarky looked around, 'who has the key?' Midgy passed him the key, 'you've got a steady hand.' The group gathered beside Clarky and the reality kicked in.

There were masses of dead in all directions. What they'd seen happen to the birds at Stead lane had happened everywhere and Midgy had been right to avoid the front street, to the extent his decision had saved all their lives.

Dead were converging from Millfield, both directions of the front street and from behind them.

Vic ran across the road, in front of the houses at Millfield Court and shouted across to the group, 'on my call run for the square.' Clarky ran across to him and Vic pointed the revolver at him, 'you've got the fucking key, Detective. Get back over there and lead our people to safety. Keep the gate open as long as you can, I'll be right behind you.' 'You fucker, Vic.' Clarky turned and returned to the group.

Vic stood on the footpath beside Millfield Court, raised his gun and fired six shots into the air. All of the dead, from all directions made towards the gunshots and, within seconds a crowd was converging on Vic's side of the road. He called out, 'now!' Clarky ran flat out along the street, the group scrambling behind him. Vic had replaced the magazine on the revolver and fired two more shots into the air, as Clarky got to the gate, further distracting the dead.

Clarky scrambled for the keys as he reached the gate, but it swung open. It was Dowser.

Clarky stepped inside and put an arm around Dowser, 'a few more on their way.'

The others made the gate and passed through and Dowser made to close the gate.

Clarky grabbed the gate, 'Vic.' He stepped back outside the gate. There were gunshots, then Vic appeared, running along the footpath, that his distraction had cleared, but dead were crossing all the way along, many stumbling and falling down the steep grass verges, on the other side of the road.

Clarky shot zombies that had got into Vic's path, just enabling him to reach the gate. He scrambled through and Dowser slammed the gate and bolted it. He just got the chain and padlock in place as the dead arrived. Dowser called out, 'we need to get out of sight.' He led the group into the square, out of sight of the dead, that were crowding outside.

Chris Dewhirst put an arm around Vic, 'thank you for what you did out there, Vic, thank you all.' He set off towards Margaret Hipsburn's house. Ted was sat on a garden wall, laughing, 'can we go again?' Midgy smiled, abso - fucking - lutely not. Come on, Ted, I'll show you where your daughter's staying. I'll sort you and Chris your own houses, later.'

* * *

Hannah, Don and Connor were half way along Ridge Terrace when the birds screamed. It was deafening and Hannah knelt on the ground, hands over her ears, 'God Almighty, Don, what's happening?'

The birds around them had taken off as the three passed, but Don could see the melee of birds taking flight in panic and injured birds scrambling away from the dead, along the road.

Connor walked ahead, keeping a safe distance from the bodies lying on the ground, then returned, 'We're going to have to run for it. The dead have caught birds. They're feeding. If they get to their feet, we're in big trouble. A couple of bites out of a crow won't fill them after days not eating.'

Don, Hannah and Connor began to run and, as they passed over the Red Lion roundabout onto the front street, the dead were beginning to stand up. They were immediately spotted and zombies began to stagger towards them, still unsteady on their feet.

They ran past dead, dodging side to side to avoid outstretched hands and as they ran, more dead were attracted towards them.

They followed the main road to an area adjacent to the council offices, where there weren't as many dead and Don spiked three zombies to buy them a few moments. Connor turned to Hannah, 'I think we'll be able to break through and make for Hollymount, Don, have the gate key ready.' Unfortunately, as they set off there were gunshots coming from the bottom of the street and Don stopped in his tracks, 'There'll be a big crowd attracted to the noise down there, look, the dead down the street have turned that way, already. There's a crowd behind us, we have to get inside somewhere.'

Hannah looked along the front street buildings, 'over there!' The three ran to the black metal gate of Breakers bar.

There was a metal tent peg where a padlock would go between two ends of a chain and Hannah pulled it out, undid the chain, unlatched the gate and they entered. She quickly closed the gate, wrapped the chain and inserted the metal peg.

Within seconds there were hundreds of dead crowding and pushing against the gate. Hannah looked at Don and Don shook his head, 'the door's locked, Hannah, we're trapped.' Hannah burst into tears, 'I'm sorry Don,

Connor.' Connor put his hand on her shoulder, 'it's ok Hannah, keep tight against the doors, I've got a crowbar in the bag.'

Zombies were reaching through the bars of the gate and fencing, trying to grab at them and Connor was reaching into the bag, when the door unlocked behind them.

The three scrambled through, falling in a heap on the stairs and Don quickly got up and closed the door behind them. A man was most of the way up the stairs and, meanwhile, at the bottom of the stairs, inside the closed doors, there was a three-way hug, in relief at the lucky escape they'd just had. Don set off up the stairs, 'come on, let's meet our saviour.'

4

Charles Andrews and Jean Allinson

Charles Andrews lay on his back in the alleyway that led from Bedlington Front Street, down to the Court house. He was laid just outside the boundary of Woolsington Court, sheltered accommodation, where the alley branches off towards the car parks, behind the front street shops and pubs.

Charles had made his way off the street, desperately seeking food. The hunger pain was his only feeling. Food was the only thing that satisfied him. There was nothing else.

For the time Charles had been this way he had found food all around, but in the last few days everything he had encountered was nothing. He could see food high up in trees, on roofs, but out of his reach and the food was noisy, constantly attracting his attention and he had wandered around, all over the area, looking for a way to reach the food he needed.

Charles' legs could not hold him up, as he reached the corner of the alley and he had gone to ground, using his last reserves of strength to roll onto his back and instinctively raise his hands under his chin.

Charles took one last look around and saw food gliding high above. He glanced towards trees and rooftops and could clearly see and hear food. Charles closed his eyes.

Time passed and Charles lay still. He could hear buzzing and he opened his eyes. Tiny morsels of food were buzzing around him. One landed in his eye and he closed his eyes again, opening his mouth at the same time.

Soon tiny amounts of food were appearing in his mouth and he closed and swallowed regularly, throughout the morning.

Charles was suddenly alerted by the sounds of fluttering and cawing, the same sounds the food was making from afar, but this was much closer. Charles opened his eyes, just as the food approached his face. He grabbed the food tight in his hands, pulled it to his mouth and bit. The food made a deafening noise, but went silent after his second bite. He chewed on the food and swallowed, then bit again.

Charles held the remnants of the food in front of his face. It seemed to be changing from food to nothing, then, after a while he was holding nothing. He dropped the non - food item to the ground and looked around.

The pain was still there. He'd had the food that normally abated this, but it was not enough. Charles needed to get to his feet. The noise being made by other food was deafening. He'd seek more food.

As Charles was standing up food crashed against him. Just like had happened before.

He grabbed, bit hard and the food became noisy. He held on, as the food struggled to escape his grip, but the hunger pain was so insatiable he held on tight and bit again, then he pulled the food closer and bit a third time. Liquid food was pouring over Charles, as he chewed, swallowed, then held his mouth against, where the fluid was escaping.

In a few minutes the pain was gone. Charles stood, holding on to the food. If the pain came back, he'd have food at hand. Food was all he needed. He stood in the alley holding the food in his arms, however, just like before, the food was becoming something else.

In a few more minutes Charles was holding nothing. He let go his grip and nothing fell to the ground. Charles sat down on the ground. The pain was gone, for now.

Charles sat for a while more, then heard the sound of something approaching and he opened his eyes. It stopped not far from him then went to ground. Charles got to his feet and walked towards the food.

As Charles got to the food his head lurched to the side and for a few moments he couldn't see or hear anything, but when he opened his eyes, the food was there in front of him again.

Charles made towards the food, then everything went dark. Charles fell to the ground and lay still.

* * *

'Come on Katie, please come out of your room.' Jean Allinson was stood outside her daughter's bedroom door, 'please Kates, I don't like being on my own. I know your upset, but it's for your own good.'

Jean and Katie Allinson had not left the house in Carisbrook, on the Beaufront Park Estate, since the dead had appeared. Her husband, Gordon was a lorry driver and had been travelling home from France, when the outbreak had gone out of control.

They had plenty food. Jean was an obsessive bulk shopper and the adjoining garage was stocked with food that could last them months, so they closed curtains, locked doors and stayed quiet for the duration, until, that is, the evening before this.

Katie had seen the dead go to ground from her bedroom window and tried to leave the house, to go to go check on her boyfriend, Callum, but mum had intervened and a bitter row ensued, Katie eventually storming off to her room.

When the birds had screamed, the next morning, Jean was terrified. She'd never heard anything like it and she had looked out and witnessed masses of birds taking off, leaving behind unfortunate ones, that had been grabbed and mortally injured. She wanted to be with Katie, not just to kiss and make up, but because she was really scared.

Jean knocked again, 'If you continue not to answer me, I'm coming in, Katie. I respect your privacy and space but ignoring me is not nice. We have to sort this out. Katie, something's happening outside. I'm really worried.' There was no reply.

Jean stood for a few more moments, then entered the room.

Jean Allinson was forty-four years old, strawberry blonde and quite attractive. She'd been married to Gordon since she was nineteen and fifteen-year-old Katie was their only child. She was wearing light grey adidas joggers, with matching top and slip-on sketchers sandshoes, that she preferred to slippers.

Jean's heart felt like it was in her mouth when she realised Katie was gone. She didn't know what to do and paced back and forth, trying to think. She knew Katie had made off to try to find Callum, 'Shit! Fuck! Shit!' Jean picked up a piggy bank, from the dressing table and threw it against the wall. Small change and broken china rattled around the room and she immediately regretted the outburst.

Callum lived in Windsor Gardens, just a few doors down from the estate entrance off the front street, beside the Community Centre and it was almost a straight walk of about a mile from their house.

Jean had no wish to go outside, but she pulled on a fleece jacket and left through the front door, carefully trying to latch it closed, with minimal noise.

There were dead on the ground, oblivious to her, still taking bites out of birds and Jean sprinted past them, making her way along the middle of the road out of Beaufront park.

By the time Jean got to the entrance to Schalkschmul Road, across the road from the court house, the dead were on their feet. The closest of them were a good distance, either way, so she made for the footpath, which led behind the court and up a long alley, towards the front street.

Jean sprinted up past Woolsington Court, but stopped in her tracks when she saw what was up ahead. One of the dead was sat, covered in blood and her daughter Katie was lying dead, beside him.

Katie had horrific bites to her left arm and the side of her neck. By the amount of blood on the zombie and the tarmac path, it was obvious she had quickly bled out.

Jean tried to scream but no sound came out of her mouth and she sank to her knees. She was almost blinded by the tears running out of her eyes and, as she looked up, the Zombie was approaching her.

Jean was frozen with fear and closed her eyes. She heard a loud crack and looked up. A young woman had struck the zombie across the head, with a rounders bat, that had a spike in its end.

The zombie hadn't died and, as it regained its balance and took another step towards her, the young woman struck it again, this time penetrating the skull and the zombie fell dead.

The young woman took Jean in her arms and held her tight. Jean sobbed, 'my baby, my little girl, oh God, my daughter.' She was shaking uncontrollably.

The young woman released her hold on Jean and looked into her eyes, 'my name is Hannah and I am with my friends Connor and Don. I'm so sorry for what has happened here, but we are in danger. You have to come with us, can you do that?' Jean nodded, 'but Katie, is she going to become…'

Don stepped forward with the spike in his hand, 'please, go with Hannah, I'll make sure she doesn't come back. We can't do any more. Dead are everywhere. I'm so sorry, I know you don't want to leave your child, but we must go.'

As the three went on ahead, Don took his spike and pierced through the young girl's temple.

Don quickly caught up the others, as they passed the court house and Jean stopped and looked back. Hannah took her hand, 'we have to go. We have a safe place. We just have to get there. Tell me your name.'

Jean took Hannah's hand, 'Jean, Jean Allinson.'

5

Breakers

The last time Don had been in Breakers was many years back, when Bedlington was the Friday night hotspot, with the disco and resident band, Stag at the Top Club and bars packed with people all the way down the front street.

Breakers was Dominique's wine bar, back then. It had become a sports bar, in recent years, with pool tables, gaming machines and motor sport décor all around.

Don, Connor and Hannah entered the bar and were greeted by four men, all sat on tall stools, at the bar. The man who had opened the door for them, was sat with the three others.

Don looked around. There was a pile of sleeping bags and heaps of canned foods, bottled water, beer, spirits, boxes of crisps, nuts, all sorts, all along the back wall and two young lads, around fifteen years old were adding more items, from their back packs. One of them took out a bottle of Famous Grouse Whiskey and a bottle of Bacardi, walked behind the bar and placed them in front of the men.

The nearest man to Don took the top off the Bacardi bottle and poured a large measure into his glass, then slid the bottle along to the others. He called out, 'Don Mason, I sed it was Don Mason, didn't ah Bobby? Remember me, Don? Ah heven't seen yee for years, Harvey Allsop, we went to school togither. We wor watchin yis oot the winda, there.'
Don took a seat at the bar, alongside, Harvey. 'I remember you, Harvey. You worked on the bins after the pits closed, didn't you?' 'aye, Don, retired noo, though.' Harvey took a drink of neat Bacardi. He was short and stocky and was wearing washed out jeans and a dirty, light blue sweatshirt, that had white paint splashes all over it, as if he'd been decorating. He had a grey beard and long greasy white hair, which hadn't been washed for some time, but had been regularly combed.

The second man took the bottle and looked up at the boy behind the bar, 'howay Happy, lad, we've got guests, give them a drink, sunner.'

The boy went into a Stella Artois box, ran across with three beers and set them down on the bar, before taking a bottle opener out of his pocket, and popping the caps. Don took a drink of beer and put the bottle on the bar, 'thanks for letting us in, I thought we were done for, down there. This is Connor and Hannah.'

Harvey looked up then took another drink of Bacardi. He pointed towards the other three men, 'Bobby Taylor ordered yar drinks in, the next fucker's Evan Ward and beside Evan is the one and ownly Willie Guthrie, the leg end of nineteen eighties Sunday league footbaal. The young uns are Happy and Robbie.

Young Happy gets his name, I'm towld, because he's such a miserable twat, nivver smiles and Robby there, well that's his name, so I'm towld. The young uns have looked after us since it started, oot there. We give them shelter in here and free access to the pool tables.

The space invaders and bandits are fucked, since the electric went doon, but they're content to just play pool. They gan oot fetching food and drink. Risky business with that fucking cunt son of Ray Donaldson on the prowl. He's knifed six of the young uns, six, isn't it Bobby?' 'aye six.' 'The fucker got in here one afternoon, killed a young lad at the back door to get in, Damon - Evan! It was Damon, that Donaldson cunt mordered, wasn't it?' Evan looked up, 'aye, Razor's son, Dennis Raisbeck, remember Dennis?'

Evan Ward was a big bloke, around forty years old. He was wearing olive coloured corduroy trousers, brown brogue shoes and a black fleece sweatshirt. His hair was dark, mousey brown and untidy, but he appeared a lot cleaner than the other men.

Harvey picked up his glass, then put it down, 'aye, aye, I remember Razor, he's the one, hey Bobby! He's the one that got filled in outside the Domino for shaggin' Ray Donaldson's lass – what's her name Bobby?'

Bobby shook his head. Harvey was clicking his fingers, as if the answer was on the tip of his tongue, but just needed the slightest help to come out, 'Willie! What did they caal that slapper that married Ray Donaldson, ye knar, the one his brothers and haff of the blokes in Millfield were fuckin?'

Willie looked up. He was tall and thin, bald headed, with a ginger beard and black rimmed national health type glasses. Willie was wearing dark jeans and a black and white Newcastle top, you know, one of the retro ones from when they won something, many, many years back. It had a large number nine on the back with the name, 'Guthrie' above. 'She was called Kylie Martin. Ray caught her upstairs in the Domino with Razor, in one of them booths. She had her coat over his lap and she was wanking him off underneath. Ray and his two brothers dragged him outside and brayed the shit out of him. His pants were still down when they got him outside.'

The Domino was the Bedlington night club of the time, on Palace Road, Bedlington Station, later called Lucifer's, Lucy's, the Palace, but closed and developed into residential flats, some years back.

Evan looked up, 'aye, that Kylie Martin. The same lass, though, Harve, the same lass could run a handrail to the moon with all the dick she's had.' Bobby chipped in, 'aye, the same lass's legs were just like this bar, aalways open,' then Willie, 'aye, the same lass was like the HMS Ark Royal, always full of semen,' then Harvey again, 'aye, the same lass couldn't get enough men 'n' cider. What was I on about again?'

One after another, the others replied, 'aye,' 'aye,' 'aye.'

Hannah spoke, 'you were telling us about Donaldson's son murdering a young lad called Damon,' 'aye, Damon and the owner, Larry. Larry tried to chuck the Donaldson kid oot and got stabbed, as well. The young uns saved us. They chased him oot with pool cues. He was after the spirits for his mam and dad, the horrible cunt. Would have knifed us all for a few bottles.' There was a commotion in the fire exit stairway and twelve young lads ran up the stairs, the last one slamming the fire door closed. The four men just took another drink.

The boys all entered the bar and stood together looking at the guests. Harvey stood up, 'these people are marras. They got into a bit of trouble oot there. What's ganning on, there, Squort?'

A young lad, Lenny Summers stepped out of the group. He was shorter than the others and very thin, blond hair and pasty complexion, with acne across his chin, 'the dead have got back up, Harv. They managed to get hold of birds and it was enough to get them on their feet.

It's carnage out there. People had come out of hiding and were scavenging shops and houses and they got overrun. There are thousands of the dead fuckers walking around looking for food. We just managed to get back, nearly lost Danny and Zac, they were stuck in the newsagents, along the road, had to fight their way through ten of the bastards.'

Some of the group were checking over the two lads in question, for bites and one of them shouted, 'they're ok, Squirt.'

Don stood up and faced the group of youths, 'Harvey was telling us you've had bother with the Donaldson boy, Alec. Well not any more. Alec Donaldson is dead. There were cheers and high fives and Squirt walked over and shook Don's hand, 'best news we've had since all this started, get in! thank you so much,' 'don't thank me, a young lad called Marty Pickering killed him. Alec Donaldson had raped and murdered his sister. Donaldson had stabbed Marty and left him for dead, but we found him. We had a confrontation with the Donaldsons and, in the end, none of the men survived.'

Squirt looked back at the group, 'Marty's alive. We know Marty, he was in our year at school. Fucking legend now.'

The group of lads went into a case of beer and passed around bottles of Stella. Two released the balls in the pool table and started racking up. Harvey walked over to Squirt and put a hand on his back, 'you can tell the lassies they can come oot.' As squirt turned Harvey held on to him and whispered, 'not Rebecca.'

Harvey sat back down and continued, 'Ray Donaldson and his in bred family deed, can't say any of us will miss the twat.'

Squirt walked over to the lady's toilet and opened the door. Eight girls walked into the bar, all between nine and thirteen years old. Harvey watched on, then turned to the three guests, 'we warn't sure yis worn't associates of the Donaldsons, so we hid the lassies. The young uns keep them safe. Thar aal survivors that thiv foond when oot scavenging. Wuddn't last lang oot there.'

Don sat back down beside Harvey and continued, 'the Donaldsons had murdered Maeve Clarke, Ian Clarke's wife. It didn't end well for Donaldson. Clarky had Ray and his son tied up inside a huge bonfire.

Marty stabbed the boy, dead and Clarky cut the body down. Clarky waited till the boy turned, then lit the fire while Alec Donaldson was eating his father alive.'

Evan looked up, 'bornt alive while being eaten. What a way to gan.'

Bobby chipped in, 'aye, the same lad, though, Evan, the same lad should have been used to being gobbled up on a regular basis, with that missus,' then Willie, 'aye, the same lad might not have been a rich man, but he always made sure his laddie had a bite to eat,' then Evan, 'aye, the same lad was a cunt of a bloke all his life but turned out to be a canny Guy in the end,' then Harvey, aye, the same lad will be immortalised in the bullying hall of flame.' The four all said 'aye' at the same time, then took a drink. Hannah sat with her hand on her brow, shaking her head, Connor chuckling alongside her.

Harvey put his glass down and turned on his stool to face Don and the others, 'this isn't our local, yi knaar, we just ended up in here when it got messy ootside. Most people had families to gan to, but us four are aal divorced. We had a couple of pints every day in the Lion and, on the day it torned bad, were just wairking home. We came up here off the street, closing the gate and door behind wis. We've got what we need here and the young uns help us oot.

They're good kids. Larry was a nice bloke. Told us we could stay as lang as we want. Wouldn't take a penny off wis for food and drink. We sat ower there watching it all gan on oot the window. We've seen yis pass here a few times, so we knar you've got a safe place, somewhere.'

Don nodded, 'you're all welcome to come back with us, we've got room for you all. Hollymount square and the farm at the bottom of Church lane. It's all secure,' 'ner we're alright here. Hey, Squort! any of you want to move in with these lot?' Squirt broke the balls on the pool table and looked up, 'We're alright here, Harv.'

Connor finished his beer and walked over to the window, 'there's still a of dead out there. If we're going, we'll have to use the fire exit out back.' Happy walked over to the stairway, went down and opened the door.

Don thanked the men and the group of young lads and the three made their way down the stairs. Happy pointed to the corner of the overgrown garden,

'Damon and Larry are over there. At rest now. There's a step ladder down there. We use it to go out. Don't move the wheelie bin on the other side. We use it to get back in. It's a tall wall.' Don shook Happy's hand, 'the offer stands, son, if things change and any of you need a place just come to Hollymount. We'll take you in.'

Happy locked up, returned upstairs and walked across to Harvey and the others. Harvey looked up, 'are they gone?' 'aye, towards the Court.' Harvey got up and walked across to the lady's toilet and opened the door, calling inside 'come on then Rebecca, they're all gone.'

A small, thin young girl, around eight years old, walked out and joined the others. Harvey patted her head, as she passed.

The girl had long strawberry blonde hair and was wearing cotton joggers, Nike training shoes and a green basketball type vest with a number three on the front and back.

She had a large, healed up wound on the top of her right arm, a deep abrasion. Where the skin had been removed was very dark red and scabbed over, but the deep teeth mark around it had healed and stood out, thick, pink scar tissue protruding around the injury, like some sort of tribal tattoo.

Rebecca's eyes were two shades of blue. The main colour was a bright, sky blue, but there was a dark, royal blue colour around the outside, of each iris, that appeared like a thin, dark ring.

Happy walked back behind the bar, picked up his beer and spoke quietly to Harvey, 'you didn't want them to see Rebecca?' 'ner, son. We divvint knaar what lies ahead. Wiv seen neeone else survive a bite, so if powers that be get wind that somebody has, she cud end up a lab rat.

Less people that knaar aboot Rebecca, the better,' 'but we haven't seen any coppers or army since the beginning, Harve.' Harvey took a drink, 'I have, though, son. I saw some at the Lion Garage, oot that window, just the other day. Black ootfits, balaclavas and automatic guns. They're after summit and if that summit is someone that's immune, they're not taking wor Rebecca.'

Connor, Hannah and Don climbed over the tall back wall and dropped down to the bin, then to the ground, coming out adjacent to the car parks that are situated overlooking the large Lidl store. There were a few dead wandering around, but none close by and Don looked around, 'we can get through the fences of the Bedlington Development area, just past the court house and cut across to Beech Grove. We'll use the park to get home, it's only a few hundred yards from where we'll come out. The alley along there leads right to the site, come on.'

The three ran along the road, that was a dead end, other than the alley and, as they entered the alley, they saw two dead, one laid out on the ground and the other, a man walking round the alley corner, away from them. Hannah ran towards the zombie and, as she rounded the corner of the alley, she saw a woman on the ground. Hannah swung the rounders bat, smashing it against the head of the zombie. The spike deflected and hadn't penetrated the zombie's skull and he stood still for a few moments, reeling. As the zombie regained its balance and stepped towards the woman again, Hannah swung the bat two handed and struck it a second time across the head. This time the spike went right into the skull and it dropped dead to the ground.

Hannah took the woman in her arms and held her tight. She was sobbing, 'my baby, my little girl, oh God, my daughter, Katie.' She was shaking uncontrollably and her face was white as a sheet.

Hannah turned and looked over her shoulder at the young girl's body.

She released her hold on the woman and looked into her eyes, 'my name is Hannah and I am with my friends Connor and Don. I'm so sorry for what has happened here, but we are all in danger. You have to come with us, can you do that?' The woman nodded, 'but Katie, is she going to become…' Don stepped forward with the spike in his hand, 'please, go with Hannah and Connor, I'll make sure she doesn't come back. We can't do any more for her. Dead are everywhere. I'm so sorry, I know you don't want to leave your child, but we must go.'

As the three went on ahead, Don took his spike and pierced through the young girl's temple.

Don quickly caught up the others, as they passed the court house and the woman stopped and looked back. Hannah took her hand, 'we have to go. We have a safe place. We just have to get there. Tell me your name.' The woman took Hannah's hand, 'Jean, Jean Allinson.'

6

The Truth about Vic Hind

Vic put his backpack, coat and the guns he was carrying onto the workbench in the wash house and made his way into the house and upstairs to the bathroom. He stripped down to his shorts and washed himself down, from a large jug and bowl Dawn had put there for him.

Dawn Todd and Vic had been together since Don had brought him to the Square.

Dawn came into the bathroom and put her arms around Vic, 'everyone ok, Vic?' 'yes, it got dangerous out there, but we made it back. We found a couple of people still alive, Margaret's brother and young Julie's dad.

Has there been anything on the radio?' 'Yes, they've been missing one of their men since yesterday. He didn't return from a search. Did you...?' 'Dawn, I had to know where they are. Clarky's onto me. He's coming over. I have to tell him. The whole community is in danger if Mcghee finds out where I am.'

Dawn stepped back from their embrace, 'they know there's pockets of survivors, I heard them talking about us, the farm, Nedderton and Bedlington Station. Mcghee is constantly asking if there's any sign of you. He called the men back in to discuss an operation and one of them said Hardman was missing.' Vic nodded, 'It'll be to extract me. The community is in danger, Dawn.'

Dawn started to cry, 'Vic, there's something else.' Vic sat on the side of the bath, and looked up, 'what else, Dawn?'

Clarky knocked on Dawn's door at around two o'clock pm. Eileen Moorhouse was with him. Dawn took them through and sat beside Vic at the dining table. Vic had a bottle of Arberlour whiskey and three glasses and Dawn went into a cupboard and took another, 'sorry Eileen, I didn't know you were coming.'

Vic poured four drinks and took a drink of whiskey, himself. He put his glass back down and sat in thought for a few moments.

Clarky took a drink of the whiskey and looked across at Vic, 'some sort of special ops, aren't you, Vic?' Vic glanced at Dawn. He'd told Dawn everything. Dawn nodded in reassurance.

Vic looked across at Clarky and Eileen and nodded, 'I'm sorry, Clarky, I should have refused to come here with Don, I've put your community in terrible danger.' 'How so, Vic?'

Vic sat back in his seat,

'Yes, I was special ops, but I'd been removed from duty, just before all this went down. There was an incident in Afghanistan, a small village where my team were sent to clear enemy insurgents, intelligence had identified. My team leader was a guy called Oliver Mcghee, a narcissistic psychopath, obsessed with his appearance, whose status and power of position had gone to his head. He was the son of a government minister, Sir Edwin Mcghee, no less. Sir Edwin had big plans for Oliver, but his son was a hot head, causing trouble wherever he went.

Mcghee was a loose cannon and when we infiltrated the village and took down the terrorists, he rounded the residents up, saying they were all involved and dragged a young woman into a house, to rape her. He'd knifed her husband. Afghanistan is bad enough with bad guys walking among civilians, but murdering and raping innocents just causes further radicalisation.

The civilians were in panic. It went from sheer gratitude for removing their oppressors to a real shit show in the time it took that fucker to pull a knife.

I wasn't going to let him rape this girl, so I entered the house and tried to reason with him. He ordered me out, so I dragged him outside and put him on the ground. That's when the others came at me, Lisle Huntly, Aaron Dunn, Corbyn Harris and Spencer Hardman.

I took a good kicking, but while it was happening, we got called for extraction. Mcghee told me it wasn't finished and I was a dead man, so, as I got up, I punched him as hard as I could, on the end of his nose. I flattened the nose, later finding out it was broken in three places. If I was going to get a bullet in the back on my next mission, he was going to live with my mark.

Bear in mind, this bloke had an obsession with his appearance, fucking sunbed tan, haircut every week, manicured nails, you know the type. To say he was pissed is an understatement.

He'd have forgiven me more if I'd shot him, but ruining his pretty boy nose?

Mcghee had private cosmetic surgery to put his nose right, but he was a real fucker. I was put on report for assaulting a superior officer in the line of battle and they spared me jail, because of my previous record.

The gardening leave I was on, was just until the dishonourable discharge went through, but I started getting phone calls from Mcghee, threatening calls and these became disturbingly frequent, like an obsession for revenge, each time from a different phone. I offered to meet with him, just the two of us, to sort it out, but he knew he couldn't take me down without his gang. He wasn't wanting a fight. Mcghee had murder on his mind.

I was living in a flat at Gosforth, when I was called back to the team. There were three suits holed up in Civic Centre in Newcastle. VIP's of some sort, important enough to risk our best men and I was put back with Mcghee and the team, with specific instructions to extract the three men and no one else.

There was a Chinook waiting on the Town Moor and we went in.

It was carnage in Newcastle. By then, there had been thousands of people bitten a day or two before and they had all turned.

We shot our way through and got to the three men in Civic Centre, but there were dozens of survivors, holed up inside, employees and security. It looked like there was no way through the crowds of dead outside, but Mcghee had a plan. He assured all the survivors inside; he would get them to safety.

Outside, there were people still trapped in cars. Dead were all over the cars, trying to get to the people inside. Mcghee went outside and started shooting car windows out. Civilians were being dragged out of their cars. I ran out to him, but it was too late. He'd made the distraction to make a break for it and ordered me to secure the rear.

The team ran on ahead with the three suits and I kept about twenty survivors in front of me, at the rear, shooting any zombie that got near, but as they got to the Town moor and over the fence, Mcghee turned and started shooting the civilians. I rolled under a car, as the dead converged on the injured people. They had no chance. He'd ordered me to the back so he could shoot me with the others, the fucking coward.

I got over the fence, further along the moor, as the team got the men to the Chinook. There were hundreds of people running from the dead, towards the helicopter, but they were being fired on by soldiers inside.

I saw Mcghee and the others try to get onto the Chinook, when the last suit was on board, but they were pushed back out and guns pointed at them and the Chinook left. The VIP's, that they had got to safety abandoned them.

It was a mistake, though. Sir Edwin Mcghee had ordered that Mcghee would be extracted with the VIP's. It was the rest of the team that had been declared expendable.'

Eileen spoke up, 'surely, Vic if these VIP's were from the establishment, they would have made room for the men who'd saved them? I always thought that in a national crisis, people like us would be needed by those at the top.'

Vic shook his head, 'people like us are nothing to them, Eileen. Even Edwin Mcghee's son didn't merit a seat beside the fuckers. Yes, in a life-or-death situation, when you're in line to take a bullet for one of them, they'll promise you the Earth as reward for their safety, but as soon as you get them there, they'll close the door in your face.
Imagine it like a game of monopoly, the guy on the other side of the table, in the Armani suit and thirty-thousand-pound watch is playing with the sports car and you are the dog. On his side of the board is all the money, all the property and all the hotels are on his property.

He has two dices and you only have one, but your dice has one spot on each of the six sides. You only have one pound on your side of the board, nothing else. The suit invites you to go first, you throw a one and land on Old Kent Road. The suit takes your pound, but, rather than declare the game won, he offers you a high interest loan to enable you to pay the rest of the rent. That's how the establishment operate.

When the three of them saw security on the Chinook, we became expendable. They were celebrating and shaking hands with each other, while Mcghee's men had guns in their faces, being pushed back towards hundreds of dead.

The five men from my team made a run for it, but Mcghee got eyes on me. He was firing at me as I ran over cars, then off the road. I scaled a fence into some allotments. There were so many dead between us, the others had to run in the opposite direction.

I hid in a shed for hours then decided to make for the coast. There was no way back to Gosforth, or Newcastle, everything was overrun. There was nothing to run back to. Newcastle was gone.

I had been nearly honest with Don, though about the zombie slime. I rounded a corner near Benton, not the Spine road, as I had told him. I ran right into a young girl. I struggled to keep her face away from me, as she tried to bite me and, as I pulled at her, trying to get my hand on my knife, I was being smeared with the slime. She was in a short skirt and her legs were covered. When she eventually lost interest, I realised they operate with the senses. Smell like them and they see you as one of them. I attached a silencer to my revolver and shot the girl, then covered myself with the slime, from her legs and lower body.

I made my way to the Spine Road, walking through hordes of dead, with the intention of walking towards Ashington, then on to Amble and north, by the coast and farmer's fields, but when I got to Horton, I could see efforts had been made to close off the Horton Road.

I went up there, hoping to find survivors and I closed up the blockade on the roundabout.

When I got to the house, where Don found me, I had decided just to stay put. I had access to Hartford Colliery to scavenge for food and a safe house, with a large horde of zombies patrolling back and forward. I really thought Mcghee and the others would just dig in somewhere safe.

I was alright there, until I saw Don, that day. I knew he'd be overrun by dead, along the road, where he was headed and I couldn't let him die, like that. I went after Don and saved him and we captured the Donaldson boy together.

It was selfish of me to come back here, but I felt I needed a fresh start. I had no idea that Mcghee was going town to town looking for me. And now he's in Bedlington.

I ran into Hardman, Spencer Hardman, a day ago, as the dead were weakening. He'd been out with two of the others and entered a house I was scavenging in Clovelly Gardens, behind the Lion garage. I immobilised him and took his radio. The other men were in the garage shop, filling bags. It was one of the few shops that had managed to get its doors closed, when this had started and the men had forced the doors.

I dragged one of the dead in from outside and held it over Hardman, inches from his face, when he came round, until he talked. Then I stabbed him through the heart and let the zombie drop on him.

They're in the Golf Course clubhouse. They've been watching the farm, us, a community at Nedderton, the lads at Bedlington Station. They're looking for me and they've got hostages.

When we got back earlier, Dawn had been listening into their comms.

They've taken two kids from farmland and they're going to approach their community tomorrow. Clarky, we need to check on the kids, here and at the farm. If any of our children have been taken, I'll have to finish this, now.' Clarky finished his drink, 'you can't do this on your own Vic, I'll come with you,' 'sorry, Clarky, but you wouldn't survive. If I fail, they will have what they want. It's not in their interest to kill anyone else and draw attention. They would just disappear.'

* * *

The kids all sat together in the barn. None of them knew why Clarky had come over to see them, but they knew he was a detective and some of them had broken some of the rules.

Clarky entered the barn with Geordie Wells and sat on a hay bale to address them all, 'right, let me just clarify here, none of you are in trouble. I know, since the dead lay down, some of you have been going out, retrieving belongings and scavenging without Geordie's permission. That's ok. What is important, here is that I can account for all of you, so I'm going to ask you all once, are any kids missing at the moment?'

There was dead silence and kids all around the barn were looking at each other.

Geordie stepped forward, 'listen kids, I know you all look out for each other, loyalty and all that, but we have reason to believe some Bedlington kids are in real danger. Please, Detective Clarke needs to know if anyone is out there.'

Will Masters took a young girl's hand. Jenny Proctor was eight years old. She was small and thin with ginger hair and she was wearing dark grey joggers and a light grey sweatshirt. Jenny had befriended Daniel Miller, a young lad, who Will had brought back to the farm, after his father had been bitten. Will walked forward with Jenny, 'it's ok, Jenny, tell Mr Clarke what you know.'

Jenny was close to tears, you know that look when a kid is dreading telling the truth, 'Daniel Miller has gone out. He's finding it hard to make friends, but he knows Jamie Jones really well, from school. Jamie came over with two air rifles. They were going out to check on the animals and to shoot rabbits and pheasants. Jamie thought if Daniel came back with food, he'd be really popular with the others.'

Will spoke up, 'Clarky, it's not that Daniel isn't well liked, he's just very shy. A lot of the kids just give him space, because he seems so uncomfortable around others. He's ok here. He's been through a lot, with his dad and all.'

Clarky thanked Jenny and addressed the rest of the kids, 'There are some very dangerous men in Bedlington. None of you are to leave the farm compound. I want you all to be on the alert. If you see anyone on your land, you tell Geordie. Geordie, lock this place down. Vic is going out to find the boys, but, until he tells us otherwise, we have to be in the alert. We need to have hourly contact on the walkies, until this is sorted.' Geordie nodded, 'will do.'

Dawn was crying, as Vic was getting dressed. He'd taken the bag that he originally arrived with and pulled out black combats, black balaclava and jumper, black boots, a chest holster and silenced revolver. He walked into the wash house and came back out with an automatic weapon; he'd gone out one evening and retrieved from the Horton Road house and he attached a sheath with hunting knife to his trouser belt. The rifle also had a silencer.

Dawn was stood by Vic's bag and he looked up and smiled, 'there's a can in the bag, there love, pass it over but make sure you don't knock the pin out.'

Dawn passed Vic the stun grenade and he tucked it into the side pocket of his combats, 'and this?' Dawn was holding a squeaking rubber dog toy, shaped like a cartoon pig, that she'd found in the bag. Vic took it and put it into the other side pocket, 'essential combat equipment, Dawn.' He grabbed some duct tape from a cupboard and put it in the same pocket as the squeaking pig

It was getting dark. Vic kissed Dawn, 'you need to get back inside, now. Dawn, I love you and I'll be back, I swear.' Dawn kissed him again. She couldn't speak.

The front door closed and Vic walked over to the front gate and took the lid off a small bin. He reached inside and took a wide paint brush in his hand and commenced painting himself all over with zombie slime. The stench was unbearable and he retched a few times.

Clarky and Eileen were at the door, as Vic passed. Clarky nodded and followed Vic to the gate, key in hand. As they got there, they heard voices, it was Don and the others. They were in the Square, behind them. Don was at Dawn's door, seeking Jamie. Clarky opened the gate and Vic left.

Clarky stood in thought for a few moments. He had to face Don and tell him what had happened. This wasn't going to be easy.

7

Bedlington Development

There were great plans for the Front Street of Bedlington, after the closure of the large Tesco store, that took up most of the space along the front of the Market Place. A shopping precinct, that would attract quality shops and businesses, a supermarket and a family pub. The plans were impressive.

Unfortunately, as months passed, then years, all that stood, other than the abandoned buildings, was temporary metal fencing. There was still talk, discussions and consultations, notices being put up, before the outbreak, but not much work had happened.

The large area behind the 'development,' once a large car park, was now a derelict, an overgrown eyesore and the front of the building, overlooking the Market place was in disrepair, marring the appearance of the Front Street.

Don, Hannah and Connor were making for the abandoned car park area, when they had run into Jean Allinson. Hannah had hold of Jean's hand and they ran along the alley, out past Woolsington Court, sheltered accommodation, past the court house and towards the large metal fence, that surrounded the abandoned car park.

There were dead coming from all directions. Some had entered the alley from the street, others, along the path Jean had taken from Beaufront park and there were dead left and right of the path that led up to the Market Place.

Connor ran past the others, knelt down and cupped both hands, 'quick, we haven't got much time.' Don put a foot into his hands and scaled over the fence. Jean did the same and Don caught her, as she rolled over, then Hannah, but Connor was surrounded. He took a couple of steps back, swinging the baseball bat at a zombie, that was in his way, then threw the bat over the fence and ran and jumped.

He was kicking and scrambling to free himself from one of the dead, that had grabbed his left leg and, as more converged on him, Don jumped up and grabbed him, dragging him over the fence by the collar of his jacket.

Connor rolled onto his back and Don put out a hand and helped him to his feet, 'you ok?' 'I think so, thanks Don.'

The dead were pushing against the fence, but luckily it was solid, black metal panels, so they couldn't see through. The group stood still and quiet and the banging against the fence soon dispelled.

Don led the group to the back entrance to the old Tesco store. It was secure and there was no way in, but they had somewhere to sit out of sight of the dead, that were milling around on the Beech Grove side of the car park, visible through the metal grated fencing that was still intact on that side.

Hannah opened her back pack and passed bottles of water and energy bars around. She put her arm around Jean, 'I know this is difficult, Jean, but we aren't far from home. We need to get fluids and food on board. It's not going to be easy, the rest of the way.'

Jean was cold and shaking. She couldn't stop crying.

Connor took off his fleece jacket and put it over Jean's shoulders, then walked across towards the Beech Grove side of the car park, keeping low. Don joined him, 'I think we'll have to lay low until dark, Connor.'

Connor nodded, 'I agree, the dead have eaten, but not enough. They're searching for food, desperate.'

Don turned to go back to the others and Connor reached out and grabbed his arm. He was crying, 'Don.' Don turned back, 'Connor, what?' Connor bent down and pulled up his left trouser leg. He'd been bitten.

Blood was running out of deep teeth marks. Connor had managed to break away and avoid losing a chunk, but the skin was penetrated deep. There was severe inflammation around the injury.

Connor kept hold of Don's arm, 'don't tell the others, they're scared enough. Make a plan. I'll help you get back, but I know it's over for me, Don.' Don put his head down, 'I'm sorry son, really sorry.' Don was so upset he felt sick, but composed himself as he returned to the others.

The group sat in the back entrance of Tesco for a good while, waiting for a gap to open up between groups of dead, that were milling around between them and their destination.

Hannah was continually reassuring Jean, but she knew something was wrong, due to Don and Connor's silence. She took a walk towards Bedlington Tyre services building, across the road from the Northumberland Arms and Verdi restaurant and looked through the fence towards the street.

There were Dead passing back and forth along the road adjacent, but there were many more on the front street.

Don joined Hannah and looked out, 'we'll never make it along the street. The park's our only way back. We'll make for the secret entrance, it's just a panel that slides to the side. We can get through quick and close it behind us.'

Hannah stood with her back to Don, arms folded, 'when are you going to tell me what's wrong, Don?' Don stood silent. Hannah turned and looked in his eyes, 'is it Connor?' Don nodded. He didn't have to tell Hannah Connor had been bitten, 'please, Hannah, he didn't want you and Jean to know.'

Hannah returned over to Jean and sat with her, trying not to glance Connor's way, but she couldn't help it. She was as upset as Don was. Hannah put her arms around Jean and cuddled her in.

Connor was sat beside Don. He picked up the Browning looked through the scope, 'so how accurate is this then, Don, could you take down that dead guy over there?' He pointed to a zombie that was clumsily walking past, about fifty yards away.' The gun was shaking, trembling in sync with his hands and arms and Don replied, 'aye, but it's a moving target, Connor. Makes a headshot harder. The gun's very accurate though, but I wouldn't recommend firing it here.'

Connor passed Don the gun, 'did I get a chance to thank you for taking me in, Don?' 'of course, you did, Connor and I'm glad you came, you're a true friend, son.' Connor nodded, 'I'm glad I came as well, Don. It was no life on my own. It took a while for me to convince myself, but the time I've had with the community…' He began shivering and folded his arms, then lay on his side.

Connor saw Hannah look at Don and spoke, 'I got bit, Hannah, I didn't want you and Jean to know, I thought it would take longer, but I don't feel good.'

Hannah quickly crawled over and knelt down beside him. She could see blood seeping out of his left trouser leg and pulled it up. She was horrified to see the leg was a dark colour, almost black from ankle to knee.

Hannah took a first aid kit out of her bag and tried to apply a dressing, but Connor held out his hand, 'leave it, Hannah, the pain, it's unbearable. I'm getting stomach cramps and my fingers.' He clenching his fists tight, so much so, his fingers cracked, then he went into a seizure. Connor's face, legs, feet, arms and hands seemed to all be in cramp.

Hannah and Don held Connor down.as his body convulsed, then his whole body relaxed and he came around.

Connor looked around, 'Don, it's getting dark, this is our time.'

Don stood up, 'we need to make for Beech Grove, around the corner and in towards the school. On the left of the park fence beside the school entrance, is a small footpath, behind the houses.

If I don't make it, about twenty yards along, there's a panel in the fence. You can't miss it. The panel slides to the left. Pass through and close it, the park is safe. There's a panel the same at the bottom of my garden.

We'll wait till there's not many dead passing, then I'll lift the fence and the three of you pass under, then we run for it. Connor, can you make it to the fence?' Connor stood up, 'I think so, Don, Hannah, can you and Jean hold the fence for Don? I'm worried I may let it drop if I go into cramp.' Hannah nodded and whispered to Jean, 'we can do this, Jean, stay close to me, just keep out of reach of the dead, they're slow. Avoid crowds of them.' Jean nodded. She was terrified, but knew it was her only chance.

Don led the way and the group sat behind a pile of rubble, about twenty feet from the fencing beside Beech Grove. They waited until a few dead had passed and Don ran forward, 'this is it.' He lifted the metal fencing and Hannah and Jean rolled under.

Dead from along the road had heard the fence rattle and, as Hannah and Jean took the fence and lifted, Hannah looked past Don. Connor wasn't there.

The fencing along the road, adjacent to the Bedlington tyre services started to rattle, noisily and the dead, that were converging on the group turned and headed towards the noise.

Don knew he couldn't do anything and he looked over and saw Connor violently shaking the fencing. Connor looked over and shouted, 'Don, make that shot for me!' Connor made one hard pull against the fence and, as it collapsed, he ran back, dragging his left leg, as around a hundred dead stumbled into the compound. Connor stood up still and straight and looked across at Don, who had raised the Browning, as the dead were getting back to their feet and walking towards him.

Hannah and Jean looked away, as Don paused for a second, overwhelmed by the assured look on Connor's face. Connor held up a hand and smiled. Don took aim again, fired the Browning and Connor fell dead to the ground.

Connor's body disappeared, immediately under dozens of hungry dead and in seconds it was ripped apart.

Hannah was in tears and Jean was now in a state of shock. Don shouldered the Browning, 'we have to go now, the gunshot will attract more.'

Jean and Hannah held the fence up for Don, then the three raced along the road, past the Coffin Chapel and into the school road. There were a few dead in their path, but Don and Hannah dispatched them and they scrambled along and down the footpath, for the panel in the fence.

Don held the panel open, as Hannah and Jean stepped into the park. He took a last look along the path as he entered, himself.

A few dead were coming along the footpath and Don slid the panel closed.

The three made their way across the overgrown park. They could see candle lights in windows at Hollymount Square and Don held the panel open for Hannah and Jean and closed it behind him as he entered the back garden.

They sat down in Don's kitchen and Don poured large whiskeys. He called for Jamie, but there was no answer. He whispered under his breath, 'must have gone to Dawn's after all.'

Don knocked back the large scotch and looked at Jean, 'please, Jean, stay here tonight. We can sort your accommodation tomorrow. We have a spare room.' Jean nodded and took a sip of whiskey.

Hannah walked with Don towards home and hugged him as they got to Dawn's house, 'I'm so sorry about Connor,' Don stood head down, 'I know, he was a good man, are you ok, Hannah?' Hannah sighed, 'I think so, I just hope they got back in one piece with Bob.' Hannah made her way into the house, as Don walked up to Dawn's front door.

Dawn had seen Don coming, through the living room window. She was dreading this.

8

The Rescue Mission

Clarky ran back to Dawn's house, after closing the gate behind Vic. She'd invited Don inside and Don was sat on the sofa, head in hands when Clarky arrived. Clarky sat down on a seat opposite, 'Dawn's told you, then?' 'just that Jamie and Daniel are missing. Do you know what's happened?'

Dawn stood up and said, 'I'll get us some drinks' and she went into the kitchen, but lent against the bench, terrified, as to how Don was going to react to what he was about to be told.

Clarky looked Don in the eyes, 'Vic isn't who we think he is, Don. He's some sort of special ops that got abandoned when Newcastle went down. Vic's on the run from his squad. The leader's got some sort of disturbing vendetta going on. Vic found out they had reached Bedlington. Dawn and him have been listening in on them. He killed one yesterday and took his comm.

When you found Vic, he was in hiding, disappeared, if you like. He had no idea the men had continued searching for him, when he agreed to come back here.

Vic ran into one of them by chance at the top end of Bedlington. He made the ops guy tell him where they were holed out, then killed him, made it look like a zombie attack. He had no idea they would take hostages. I think Vic wanted us to go out clearing the dead, so he could slip away and take them out. Our rescue venture, today has given them the opportunity they've taken.

The boys had gone out without permission, Don. Jamie only wanted to take Daniel shooting with the air rifles. He knew Daniel was struggling to settle in at the farm. They must have run into the op's guys, on the farm land. Vic told me they'd be coming here to exchange the kids for him, in the morning, so he's taking it to them, tonight, instead.

Don, Vic is a ghost, special forces. He knows these fuckers intend to kill him so he's hitting them first. He's confident that if he fails and they kill him, they'll let the boys go.'

Don looked up, 'I can't take that chance, Clarky, you know it.' Clarky nodded, 'I know, Don.'

* * *

It wasn't long before Vic ran into dead. A large group, most of them covered with dried blood and feathers, walked past, glancing at him, but they ignored him and walked on towards the Black Bull pub. There were a lot of dead around and Vic slowly walked along the front street, crossed the road, beside the Red Lion pub and walked down past the Salvation Army, towards the golf course.

Vic knew the drill. There were four men, two would be patrolling and two inside with the prisoners. It was obvious one would be out of sight, overlooking the gate, taking down any stray dead and there would be one man out of sight, overlooking the entrance to the base, probably down by the first tee box, or somewhere along the first fairway, in sniper range.

When Vic reached the bottom of the road, near the golf course, he stopped and took a rolled-up length of rope out of the bag. There were around twenty dead nearby, on the road into the Hartlands and he picked one out, a really big fellow, curly ginger haired, wearing grey shell suit bottoms and a massive combat jacket. He was over six feet and around twenty stone. His dirty white trainers were about size fourteen.

The big guy's front was covered with blood and feathers and he was slightly docile, but Vic knew a guy that size would still be hungry.
Vic quickly made a loop in the rope and slowly wandered alongside the big, dead guy. He whispered under his breath, 'I'm going to call you Bunter,' then lassoed the rope over his head and gently pulled the knot tight.

Vic walked a distance ahead and carefully tugged at the rope. Bunter reluctantly stumbled his way along, behind and Vic guided him to the edge of the overgrown golf course driving range fencing and tied the rope to a lamp post.

Vic made his way down the twenty acres footpath, found a gap in the fence half way down and entered the driving range, crossing it, into the car park. He quickly ran down to the bottom of the car park and passed through an open gate, coming out a way down from the first tee.

He crossed through an area of trees, coming out adjacent to the back of the eighth tee and he got down and crawled around the tee box and behind some trees.

Vic lay on his stomach, carefully and slowly scanning left and right. It seemed like there was nothing there, then he saw a small light, half way along the first fairway, beside a small pond and he thought to himself. 'That's where I'd be.'

Vic crawled back across to the bottom of the eighth tee box and then passed along a path that came out beside the ninth green. He ran to the top of the ninth fairway and made his way across the overgrown eighth green. The grass was just over ankle length, fine and soft and it had gone to seed. The flag was still in the green. He passed through some trees and made his way around, coming out among the trees separating the first and eighteenth fairways.

Passing one tree at a time, Vic crawled through the tree line, making his way towards the back of the pond. He eventually got to a large conifer and rolled on his back, checking over the silenced revolver. He slowly crawled the last twenty yards, or so, to the back of the pond and saw one of the men, completely in black, laid on his side, watching over the clubhouse. He had an automatic rifle, scoped and laid with its barrel across a small tripod and there was a small kit bag at his side.

There was a lamp on in the clubhouse, but Vic couldn't make out people inside. He took the revolver, aimed with both hands and fired.

Corbyn Harris was still holding the cigarette, that had given his position away to Vic and he hadn't moved when the shot hit him. The back of his head was like a crater full of splattered brains, as Vic scrambled around the pond and took position beside him. He quickly removed Harris's coms and put the earpiece on.

There was no communication going on, so Vic quickly made his way back along the tree line and crossed the overgrown fairway, making his way back to the car park, out of sight of the clubhouse.

Vic returned to Bunter, beside the Twenty Acre field. He slowly approached from the rear and stood beside him. Bunter looked disinterested and confused, as to why he could not walk away and repeatedly took a step forward, then back as the rope tightened.

Vic gave the rope some slack, then put his rifle between Bunter's feet the next time he stepped forward and Bunter fell to ground. Vic quickly pulled out the squeaking pig and duct tape from his pocket, grabbed Bunter's right foot and taped the pig to the sole of his size fourteen trainer.

Bunter was waving his arms around, in an effort to regain a position, from which he could get back to his feet and Vic rolled to the side, allowing him to do so.

Vic took the rope and led Bunter into the middle of the road. Every time Bunter put his right foot down, the pig squeaked, but better than this, Bunter followed the sound, so each squeak drove him forward, seeking the source of the unusual sound.

Vic used the rope to guide Bunter in the direction of the golf course and Bunter set off, a step, then a squeak, step, squeak. Vic carefully took the rope from Bunter, wrapped it up and put it over his shoulder.

He quietly and slowly moved towards the driving range fence and climbed over. He watched as each squeak Bunter made attracted dead from the Hartlands and soon around fifty were slowly walking towards the golf course, alongside Bunter.

Vic made his way along the shadows, adjacent to the groundsmen's outbuildings and climbed up on a low, flat roof, from where he could see the entrance. He could hear Bunter slowly making his way along the road, with others joining him, then he heard a voice on the comms, 'a lot of dead making their way along here. I don't know what it is, but there's a squeaking noise coming from them. If they turn into the entrance, I'm going to need some help, here.'

Mcghee's voice came on the comm, 'Harris stay put, Huntly will support, Dunn at the gate - Dunn, Huntley's on his way.'

Vic climbed down and hid behind hedges, beside the small car park at the entrance, as Huntly came along the covered walkway from the clubhouse to the entrance. He saw Dunn emerge from a small path to the right of the main entrance, beside a small building, with a white garage door and the two stood together holding assault rifles and looking along the main road. Huntly spoke into the comm, 'too many dead sir, we need to go silent, we're coming back inside.'

The stun grenade went off and both men were laid out on the ground. Vic ran over, shot them both twice in the chest, turned and ran back about fifty yards to the bottom car park.

Vic removed the magazine from the revolver and checked there were still rounds available. He checked the assault rifle, then made for the clubhouse. He kept tight against the wall,

along the covered walkway and glanced around the corner. The door was open. He looked down, towards the first tee box and could see two figures, stooped down behind a hedge. He closed his eyes and shook his head.

Vic kept tight to the wall, dropped the rifle and held the revolver in both hands. He knew Mcghee would have heard the stun grenade and would be ready, but the priority was to secure the boys and he knew his next move was a huge risk.

He spun through the door and entered, aiming the revolver in front of him. There were two boys inside, with black hoods over their heads, but Mcghee wasn't there.

Vic heard a sound and immediately knew where Mcghee was. He held out his hands and dropped the revolver.

Mcghee was stood in the doorway behind Vic. He'd climbed onto the roof on hearing the stun grenade and dropped down behind, when Vic had entered the room. He laughed, loudly, 'Jesus, Hind, you really thought I'd leave the door open for you? You fucking amateur.' Vic turned and faced him, 'bravo, Mcghee, you disturbed cunt. You've got what you want, now let the boys go.'

Mcghee laughed again, 'let the boys go? you were always the sentimental one, Hind. No respect for the spoils of war, to the extent you would disfigure one of your own men. Maybe one of these boys will make up for that. What do you say, Hind? Maybe I shoot you in the face now and give one of these boys the fucking, that bitch terrorist should have got?'

Vic looked him in the eyes, 'she was no terrorist Mcghee, you know it. An innocent civilian, but that doesn't matter to you, does it?'

Mcghee pointed the gun at Vic's face, 'any last words, Hind?' Vic smiled, 'yes, the surgery to your nose has made you look like Frankenstein's monster, you ugly cunt.'

Vic closed his eyes and a shot rang out. Mcghee gasped and fell to the ground, dropping his revolver.

Vic opened his eyes and Clarky was stood outside, with Don. The two ran inside and quickly took the hoods off the boys' heads.

Don called out, 'Vic, they aren't our boys.'

Vic picked up Mcghee's revolver, flicked on the safety and threw it to Don.

Two boys were sat at a table that had been carried over to the bar at the back of the room, both the same age group as Jamie and Daniel. Vic could hear intermittent squeaks from outside, 'we have to go.' Don and Clarky led the boys out and over the eighteenth green and Vic looked down at Mcghee.

The shot had gone through Mcghee's back and probably caused trauma to the spine, because Mcghee could not move. The shot had also attracted the dead from the entrance.

Mcghee pleaded with Vic, 'you have to help me, Hind, I'm badly hurt, I can't run. Help me now. I'm your superior officer, Hind.'

Vic looked down at him, 'not any more, Frankenstein.' He laughed out loud, 'you called me a fucking amateur, when you had a gun on me, but from the vantage point of the roof of this building you didn't make two civilians, twenty yards along the path, who may as well have come with the local colliery band. Fucking special forces team leader? My fucking arse! This team has carried your over privileged arse from the off, Mcghee and look where it's got four good men.

You went after the wrong man, Mcghee. I didn't abandon you out there. I ran for my life from you. People like your fucking father abandoned you to be eaten by the dead and you scoured Northumberland to kill the man who once tried to knock a bit of sense into you. You sad, sad mother fucker.'

Vic dragged Mcghee to the doorway and laid him on his back, with his head outside the door frame. He could hear the squeaking but it wasn't coming closer. Dead were just milling around the walkway, waiting for stimuli of any sort and, until Bunter decided to walk on, his under - foot squeak was all that attracted them, so Bunter stepped, bumped into others and stepped back, continually repeating the squeaking that had drawn the group of dead, who hadn't been able to get to the food on offer at the entrance.

Vic closed the door against Mcghee's neck, so he was laid face up and he wrapped the rope tightly between Mcghee's legs, then tied it tight to the door handle, outside, so only Mcghee's head was exposed and the door could not be opened, outward. Mcghee lay, sobbing, looking up to the dark sky, as Vic walked over to the walkway. Mcghee tried to pull his head back inside, but his arms and legs were limp and the rope just pulled tight against his groin. The bottom of the door and frame was tight against the sides of his neck and all he could do was lye there.

Bunter had just got to the front of the group of dead and he stepped forward as Vic came into view. Vic looked at Bunter and smiled, 'supper's up, thanks, Bunter.' Bunter's foot squeaked, as he stepped towards Vic.

Vic picked up the assault rifle, then disappeared across the overgrown fairways, leaving Mcghee, who was, by then hearing an intermittent squeak getting louder and louder. Vic had just got to the pond, when the screaming started and he picked up Harris's rifle, revolver and bag and ran off.

Bunter had gratefully accepted his reward for helping Vic out. Mcghee's face and head was on Bunter's menu and Bunter was very hungry.

The men stopped in the golf course car park and Vic joined them a few minutes later. They could hear Mcghee screaming.

Don put a hand on the two boys' shoulders, 'tell me your names and where you're from.' A boy around thirteen years old spoke, I'm Aaron, Aaron McDonald and this is Michael Houseman. Aaron had long dark hair, tied back and was wearing grey combat trousers and a charcoal Adidas hoodie, with black adidas trainers. Michael was a bit smaller than Aaron;

thick curled blond hair and he was wearing black Nike shell bottoms and a light grey Nike hoodie. He was wearing black Nike trainers, that looked brand new, which he'd earlier taken from an abandoned house in the Hartlands, near where a row of houses had burned to the ground, recently.

Aaron continued, 'We're from Nedderton. We have a camp on the farm land. We were out scavenging, when the dead had gone down and these men took us. They had guns. They were going to visit the farm tomorrow. They said they're looking for a man and they would let us go when they get him. I told them he wasn't at our camp, but they wanted to see for themselves.' He looked at Vic, 'you're the man they were looking for, aren't you?'

Vic nodded. He put a hand on the boy's shoulder, 'the stuff that man said about raping you was bullshit, son. He only wanted me to think that as I died. He would have let the two of you go. Don't have nightmares about it. Listen, your safe, now. We're going to take you home. There're a lot of dead around, so we'll go by fields, you lead the way. I promise we are friends.'

Aaron looked at Michael and he nodded.

The five of them cut back across the long grass, on the golf course, then set off along the eighteenth fairway. Mcghee had gone silent, but the lamp was still on, inside and they could see a crowd of dead, trying to get into position around Bunter, but with little success. Bunter was knelt over Mcghee, tucking in.

The group climbed over a length of fencing, one of the few that wasn't covered in hedging and crossed the main road, half way down towards Hartford Hall and got onto farmland, through another hedge covered wooden fence, that a car had crashed through.

As they neared Nedderton there was a voice on a walkie that Clarky was carrying. 'Clarky, do you read?' Clarky took the walkie from his belt, 'yes, Geordie.'

There was a pause then Geordie spoke again, 'Clarky, we've got a big problem, here. Ken Martin has turned up at Millfield and he's sent a message. He said he's got our boys. He found them shooting on the fields above Humford. He was on his way here, anyway, but he's taken the boys as hostages. He wants you and Paul Dawson in exchange for the kids. He said he wants an eye for an eye for the murder of his sister and Craig Thompson.

There's about ten of them, all armed with shotguns. Sharon Thompson is with them. She led them here. I don't know what she's told them but they're gunning for you and Paul. They've given us until nine am tomorrow. They said they will do the exchange on the field, outside the Donaldson house. They said if anyone is seen in Millfield before then, the kids will be shot. The note says that Ian Clarke and Paul Dawson must be outside Ray Donaldson's house, alone at nine am or the boys will be shot.'

The men were silent, as they neared the Nedderton community. Aaron stopped half way along the road, 'wait here. If strangers approach, they'll shoot first, ask questions later.'

Five minutes later Aaron returned with two men and a woman. Michael ran to the woman who embraced him. The two men walked over. One of then offered a hand and shook hands with all three, then the other man did the same. The first man stepped back, 'I'm Ed and this is Eustace.'

Ed was around seventy years old, white haired, but strong looking. He had a white beard and was wearing a navy boilersuit. Eustace was younger, about early fifties, bald head, clean shaven, with silver rimmed glasses and he was also wearing a navy boilersuit, that was open, revealing a black sweatshirt, with a white Guinness logo. The two men were both wearing wellies with the legs of the boilersuits tucked into long wool socks.

Ed spoke again, 'young Aaron said you saved the boys. Some bad men had kidnapped them, looking for one of you.' Vic stepped forward, 'they were looking for me, a vendetta. I'm sorry the boys got dragged into something like this. I'm Vic Hind, these are my friends, Don and Clarky.'

Ed nodded, 'listen, we keep ourselves to ourselves, here, but you can stay the night. The dead are up and about, desperate to feed. It's safe here.'

Don looked at the others, Clarky shook his head, 'I'm sorry Ed, but we have the same problem you have just had. It was no coincidence we stumbled on your boys. We were looking for two of our own.

Unfortunately, they are being held at Millfield by someone else and the kidnapper wants two of our men in exchange.

We had an incident involving a family member of his, who tried to take over our community. It ended badly for them all, but the brother of one of them has been sought out and he's come over from New Hartley with armed men. We have to get back, Ed. They said we have to go at nine o'clock tomorrow morning to meet them in Millfield. We have to get back and decide what we're going to do.'

Ed put a hand on Don's shoulder and looked him in the eye, 'you don't know how grateful we are to you for saving our boys. We've lost enough people to the dead. Thank you, Don, gentlemen. I am in your debt.'

The men shook hands once more and Don, Clarky and Vic made the fields, towards home.

9

Sharon's Errand

Cynthia Dodds and Amanda Blewitt had come to terms with what had happened to their husbands. Both knew what atrocities their husbands had been involved in, with Alec Donaldson, Although Amanda had kept the contents of the footage of Gary Blewitt, Craig Thompson and Abe Gardener from the others.

Unfortunately, Sharon Thompson was still traumatised and couldn't settle. She couldn't come to terms with what Paul Dawson had done to her husband and, the more she obsessed with this, the more she convinced herself of Craig's innocence from any wrongdoing. She saw Paul Dawson as a cold-blooded murderer, who had decapitated her husband, when he was surrendering and she wanted revenge.

The night that the dead had laid down, conversations had become heated.

The three women were at the dining table, sharing snacks and a bottle of wine, when the conversation again returned to Sharon's husband, 'he did nothing wrong and that bastard still hit him with the machete. We can't let this go. They'll be back over. Just give it time, they'll be back over and they'll kill us, just like they did Gary.'

Cynthia was shaking her head, 'Don Mason is good for his word, Sharon. You heard him say we were alright to stay here, just this morning.'

Amanda spoke up, come on Sharon, you know the men were the instigators of what happened at Hollymount. It was Ray Donaldson's fault. What would Craig have done if Mason and the others had surrendered? Do you think the men were going to let Mason, Clarke or any of the others live? Craig would have done the same to that lad, if Ray had told him to. He was like a fucking lamb following Ray. I'm sorry, Cyn, but the others were, too.

How long before Alec Donaldson would be raping the Hollymount children?

What happened there, happened for a reason. The trouble came to an end and we've been spared and I thank God for that, because I know, Sharon, Ray wouldn't have spared any of them and you know that too.'

Sharon stood up and threw a drink in Amanda's face, 'fuck you, Amanda and fuck you too Cynthia.'

Amanda dived over the table and grabbed Sharon by the hair, knocking over the glasses, snacks and wine bottle. She rolled over and pulled Sharon into the middle of the kitchen floor, slapped her hard, three times across the face and pinned her down on her back, 'fuck me and fuck Cynthia! Well fuck you and your fucking self - pity!

We're walking over fucking eggshells for you, you fucking bitch and, what for? All we get in return is your fucking constant winging, constant fucking paranoia. Don't you think if the devils of Hollymount Square wanted us dead, it just may have fucking happened before now?

What are they waiting for? The dead are lying down outside, motionless. They've had a clear path all fucking day. No Sharon, you need to change the fucking record, because before, you were getting on my nerves. Now you've gone beyond that.

You fucking shut up about fucking Craig, fucking Sammy and fucking Gary. I don't want to hear it anymore.'

Amanda got to her feet, took a tea towel and wiped her face, as Sharon scuttled along the floor, out the kitchen and ran upstairs.

Cynthia picked up the bottle of wine, that had been knocked over, took off the lid and shared what was left into the glasses Amanda had picked back up.

Cynthia knelt down and picked up the bowl, that had been holding the crisps and nuts and used her hand to brush up the spilled food, then she stood up, tipped it into the bin and put the bowl into the kitchen sink.

She sat back down and looked across at Amanda, 'that's been coming for a while.' Amanda sat back down and took a drink, 'she knows fuck all, fuck all and I'll tell you now, Cyn, if this continues, she's out of here.'

Cynthia Dodds nodded. She wasn't the fighting type, but Sharon had been getting on her nerves too.

At around four in the morning there was a noise downstairs, like a door banging. Amanda sat up in bed and shook Cynthia, who was lying beside her, 'someone's outside.' Cynthia got out of bed and looked out of the window. A lot of birds had appeared during the day and they had been perched on rooftops, lamp posts and trees, but it was pitch dark. It wouldn't be birds.

Cynthia could see nothing. She went downstairs and found the front door wide open. It had been blown against the wall by the breeze.

She closed the door and carefully checked the whole downstairs. No one was there and she went back upstairs and checked all the rooms.

Cynthia went back into the bedroom and sat on the bed. She looked at Amanda, 'Sharon's gone. She left the door wide open.' Amanda sat up, 'she could have cost us our lives, the stupid bitch. Where has she gone?'

* * *

Sharon made her way along Millfield, onto the Front street and down the Picnic Field bank. It was after four o'clock in the morning and very dark, but she could make out the bodies, laid out on the road and she knew to keep a wide berth.

She could hear occasional disgruntled cawing from the birds, that had congregated all over and roosted in close proximity to one another, for the night, but it was so dark, she couldn't see the birds.

She'd imagined the walk to New Hartley would take around two hours, but hadn't given any thought to the number of dead she would have to make her way through, so she slowly moved side to side, avoiding getting close. She also had obstacles of abandoned cars, she couldn't see past, so it was a very slow process.

It took Sharon over an hour to reach the Horton Road barrier of cars and she climbed over bonnets and onto the road. There was a clear stretch of road ahead, so she made good ground, but she was horrified, when she got near the first house, by the road.

There were hundreds of dead, all laid out on their backs, covering the road for around a quarter of a mile. There was no way past, other than to enter the fields.

Sharon found a gap in the hedge and walked across to the back of the field and made her way along, adjacent to the roadside, climbing wire fences, along the way.

Fields where horses had once been kept were empty and it was silent and dark.

Sharon sat down in a field, around fifty yards from the cemetery. She could see an old stone wall and the tops of some tall gravestones. The stone church stood proud in the background, even in bad light.

It had been heavy going walking through long grass in the gloom and she decided to wait an hour, or so, until it got a bit lighter. She opened the bag she was carrying and took out an orange Lucozade Sport and a bar of Galaxy chocolate and sat with her back resting against a tree.

Sharon had dozed off and she woke up with a start. It was light and there was a lot of bird noise. When she looked around, there were birds everywhere. Black birds, of all kinds were perched on power cables, telephone wires, trees, lamp posts, hedges and fences and there were thousands gliding around in the sky.

Even the tree Sharon was sitting at, was covered in birds, looking down at her. A couple of birds flew past, as if intending to land beside her, then took flight, when she stood up.

Sharon looked around. The Shoes pub wasn't far along the fields. She shouldered the bag and made her way towards the Shoes.

When she climbed the fence into the Shoes entrance road, Sharon looked around. There were dead lying around the entrance road, but nowhere near the amount she had seen earlier.

She made her way to the blockade of cars beside the Spine Road roundabout, climbed up onto a car bonnet and looked across. There were dead laid out everywhere. And one man walking towards her. He was around thirty years old, five feet ten, brown hair and was wearing a Weird Fish Tee shirt, that was like the Pink Floyd design, with the logo, 'carp side of the moon,' covered in dried blood. The zombie was wearing washed out denim shorts and slip-on navy trainers with no socks. He had blood down his front and was holding a dead fox, which he dropped as he neared Sharon. His face had been badly bitten and Sharon could see bites on his legs and arms. She was terrified.

Sharon jumped down onto the roundabout side of the blockade and looked along the road. There were spaces between the dead bodies, so she quickly worked her route out and started walking, quickly.

The man followed, stumbling against the bodies that Sharon was avoiding.

The roundabout had been a continual walk, round and round, for the thousands of dead that had made it there, like a zombie trap. It was slimy, underfoot and stank. Sharon was careful not to go too fast and cause herself to slip onto bodies.

The slip roads on an off the roundabout from the Spine Road had been constantly crowded by dead, creating a one-way horde on each road, with no way back out.

The roads along to the Cramlington and Newsham roads had been blockaded and so there were thousands of dead for Sharon to get past. Sharon carefully and slowly, negotiated her way around bodies, all laid out the same.

There were thousands of birds perched on the fences, as if an audience had gathered to see if the pursuing dead guy catches the living woman, but she ignored this and climbed up onto the next blockade of cars.
She climbed over and sarcastically waved at the dead man, who was still clumsily making his way across the roundabout.

The next road was clear. Whoever had made the blockade had meant it to be secure and had finished all the dead between roundabouts.

There was no living around, though and so Sharon made her way to the next blockade.

Sharon climbed up onto the blockade of cars, then quickly crouched down. There was dead walking around, around ten of them. They had blood down their fronts, so had eaten and when Sharon looked around, she could see dozens of rabbits coming in and out of the roadside verges. Rabbits must have got too close to some of the dead, before they'd gone down. These dead had a food source and had managed to survive.

Sharon hid behind the cars and watched the ten dead pass. There were four women, five men and a young boy, all with horrific bite injuries. They responded to every noise around them and the roosting crows cawed as they passed, almost as if taunting them from their safe positions.

Sharon let them round the far end of the roundabout, then crossed the barrier, onto the roundabout.

The path was a lot clearer than the last one, so she ran across.

As she reached the far side a zombie sat up. It had fresh blood on its face and a rabbit was laid at its side, making a high-pitched screeching sound and its body was jerking, as it tried to hang onto life.

Sharon had never heard any sound come from a rabbit. This was horrific. There was a large bite out of its side and it soon died.

Sharon tried to run around the man, as he got to his feet, but he fell forward. She screamed with terror, as the zombie grabbed at her, trying to get a tight hold and she struggled, punching and kicking him.

The other dead had heard the commotion and were making their way back towards her and, as the zombie that had hold of her reeled back, tripping over a laid-out body, the others converged on them and Sharon went to ground.

Sharon was on her knees and scrambled to make for a gap, finding herself a few feet from the large group. None of the dead had hold of her, so she crawled along, as quickly as she could, scrambling over the top of one of the laid out dead. It immediately grabbed the bag that Sharon was carrying, that had bumped against its hands. She desperately struggled to pull the bag off her shoulder, but it was being pulled tight.

The strap gave way and Sharon let the bag go.

The group of dead were virtually on top of Sharon again, as she scrambled to her feet and she ran for the next blockade. Cars were piled up in front of her and she slipped down a number of times, scrambling back to her feet, each time.

Sharon jumped up against a Range Rover car, grabbing the windscreen wiper and then scrambled onto the bonnet. She got to the roof of the car, just as the dead bumped against the blockade and she ran over a second car, then slid down to the other side.

Sharon was on the road that leads down to the Keel Row Pub, then New Hartley and Seaton Deleval. There were dead laid out on the road, like previous, but she'd had enough of main roads. She climbed a wooden fence and entered the field.

Sharon made her way into the middle of the field and stopped and looked back. The group of dead were bumping against the blockade of cars, still looking for the meal they had missed out on.

She knelt down and cried. There was no safe way back, so if Ken Martin wasn't at New Hartley, she had no idea what she would do?

Sharon had a sudden panic. She'd been attacked and she was sore from head to toe, but had she been bitten?

She quickly ran her hands all over her body. There were no injuries. She put her head in her hands and cried with relief.

After a few more minutes Sharon composed herself and made her way through the fields, past the Keel Row pub and towards New Hartley.

Sharon came out onto the main road with about a mile and a half to go. She'd been to Ken's house before, a few years back.
Ken and Mary had held a birthday party for Kylie, but Ray had spoilt it, causing trouble. He never could hold his drink, but, although Ken wasn't keen on Ray, or his brothers, he was fond of Sharon and Craig. He and Craig had played football in the same team and travelled abroad together a few times, when they were younger.

It was Craig's friendship with Ray that had driven a wedge between them, but they had never fallen out. Ken had married and moved away and they hardly saw each other, after that.

One thing about Ken, though. he was a tough bloke. A man not to be messed with and Sharon was sure he'd help her, when she told him about Kylie and Craig's 'murders.'
Sharon made her way along the road into New Hartley, it was much the same as Bedlington had been. Dead lying all over. Thousands of birds roosting at every vantage point.

She passed the first mini roundabout, then took the next left, towards Maple Court.

Sharon stood outside the blockade, that was preventing her from entering Maple Court.

Cars were piled up, but covered in grease, that had been painted on the body work and there were bricks piled up under cars, with no gaps, that a person could crawl under.

She stood, arms folded, wondering what to do.

'Let me know if you work it out.' Sharon turned and Ken Martin was stood behind her, with three men, all carrying shotguns. He was tall and dark haired, muscular and quite good looking. He was unshaven and wearing dark jeans, black trainers and a black tee shirt, under a black leather motorbike jacket. One of the men took a device out of his pocket and pointed it at a white van. The door unlocked and Ken opened the side door.

The panel on the other side of the van had been cut out and the men passed through into Maple Court. Sharon followed.

Maple court was tidy, gardens well maintained and there were more men milling around, house to house, all carrying shotguns. Sharon followed Ken to one of the houses and he invited her in.

Sharon cried with relief and Ken took her in his arms, 'Sharon, you've come here from Bedlington, a pretty hazardous journey. Something's wrong.' He took a bottle of Jaimeson's whiskey and poured a glass, then bent forward and pushed it along the coffee table, towards her.

Sharon took a large drink and put the glass back down, 'I'm sorry, Ken, Kylie's dead.'

Ken stood up, 'Kylie.? How, Sharon.' Sharon looked down, 'she was murdered, Ken, murdered by a gang at Hollymount Square. They killed Kylie and all the men.

They murdered your nephew, Alec, Ray and Craig. A man called Paul Dawson took a machete to Craig. Craig had done nothing.

They killed Jimmy, Mick and Gary and the man who killed Kylie, Ian Clarke, murdered Sammy Dodds and Abe Gardener, as well.'

Ken went into a cupboard and took another glass, half filling it with whiskey. He took a drink, 'I know Ian Clarke, copper?' 'yes, bent copper, though. Murderer. He burned Ray and Alec alive, the bastard and my Craig. He had surrendered, then that maniac Paul Dawson beheaded him.'

Sharon looked around, 'Mary, where's Mary?' 'Lost her at the start, Sharon. She was bit by one of those things, before we knew how dangerous they were. Listen, Sharon, I'm going to have to talk with some of the lads, here about our Kylie. We can't let this go.'

Sharon almost smiled, but put her head down and pretended to cry, 'I…I don't want to be on my own, Ken.' She took his hand and looked him in the eyes.

Ken had always been fond of Sharon. She was attractive and always friendly and as she stepped closer, he put his arms around her. Sharon's clothes were stinking, but he didn't mind, she wouldn't have them on much longer.

They kissed and he led her up the stairs. As they entered the bedroom, Sharon kicked off her shoes, then Ken pushed her onto the bed. He quickly yanked off Sharon's leggings, top, bra and panties and threw them out of the room.

Ken threw his trousers to one side and he lifted Sharon's legs up to his shoulders. Ken knelt on the bed with his cock pressing against Sharon's vagina, 'I've always wanted to fuck you Sharon, you fucking know it as well.' Sharon smiled, nervously and nodded.

She'd just seen his cock and it was very big and she gasped as he pushed hard against her and it slowly squeezed deep inside her. Sharon soon orgasmed and Ken pounded her hard, then withdrew his cock and fired a huge load of ejaculate all over her breasts and stomach.

He got off the bed and walked through to the bathroom, picked up a toilet roll and threw it to her, as he came back into the bedroom, 'clean yourself up, your covered in cum. It's… it's been a while.'

Ken pulled his trousers back on and left the bedroom, with a huge grin on his face. He stopped in the doorway and turned towards her, 'Mary's clothes are in the wardrobe. Wear what you want.'

Sharon stood back from the bedroom window, looking over the close, as Ken walked outside and called the men together. She could hear him speaking, 'My sister, her family and friends have been murdered in

Bedlington. The woman that's just arrived here, Sharon Thompson, is a friend. Her husband was murdered in cold blood.

Two men are responsible. Their names are Ian Clarke and Paul Dawson. I know Clarke, but not Dawson. I can't let this lie.

I'm going over to Bedlington to sort this out. The two men responsible will take a bullet for this. Is anyone with me?'

There were twelve men congregated. The all put their hands up. Ken looked around, 'arm yourselves, we leave first thing tomorrow morning. We'll use the fields to Hartford Colliery and the woods to Bedlington to avoid the dead. Meet here six am. I've got stuff to do for the rest of today. Sharon looked around the close. There were women in the doorways of all the houses. One was heavily pregnant.

The men were smiling and chuckling, as Ken made his way back to the house. Sharon smiled and sat back on the bed. She was still naked. And her skin was sticky around her chest where she'd wiped away a lot of semen. She lay on her back and whispered under her breath, 'Paul Dawson, you'll get yours, soon.'

She heard someone on the stairs and sat up. Ken walked back into the room and closed the door behind him. He took off his shirt and trousers and knelt on the bed beside Sharon, 'if I do this for you, for Craig, what will you do for me?' She looked in his eyes, 'anything.'

Ken took his big, hard cock in his hand and offered it, towards Sharon's face. It was the biggest cock she'd ever seen, probably twice the size and thickness of Craig's, if not more.

Sharon took it in both of her hands and put her mouth over it. Ken roughly grabbed her hair and pulled her head forward, nearly choking her with the cock and she gagged, but kept taking it in her mouth, back and forth, as deep as she could, until he pulled it out and guided her onto all fours.

It was going to be a long day for Sharon. Ken had a disturbing sex addiction, just like his sister and nephew and this was heightened by Sharon's vulnerability. What had been intended as an exciting way to get Sharon's hooks into Ken, was soon to become endurance.

Ken's group had found no female survivors, to date and there were no available women at the close, so he'd got by through wanking to porn magazines, every night. But the real thing was right in front of him offering her honey pot up to him, right now. Yes, Ken had some real catching up to do.

10

Leverage

Sharon got out of bed and looked out of the window. It was getting dark and it was quiet outside, other than thousands of birds. Perched outside the close on rooftops, walls and trees, relentlessly cawing.

Ken was asleep and she tiptoed out of the room, being careful not to wake him in case he decided to fuck her again. Apart from twenty minutes or so, between erections, Ken had pounded Sharon all afternoon and evening and she was tired and sore.

She pulled on Ken's tee shirt, went down to the kitchen and found some cereal bars in a cupboard and there was a crate of diet coke on the bench. She opened a coke and sat at the table. The house was nice inside, Mary had been one of those women who kept the house immaculate and, after she'd died, Ken had made sure the house stayed the way she'd have wanted.

Sharon finished the snack and wandered into the sitting room. There was a long dark brown, leather settee and matching chair, smoked glass coffee table and a massive television installed on the main wall.

She looked at a Dallas K Taylor seascape oil painting of Seaton Sluice Harbour. It was stunning, then she saw a framed photograph, on a unit in the corner of the room, with Ken and Mary together in better times.

Sharon sat on the settee and fell asleep.

It was very dark, when Sharon woke. She could hardly see in front of her, but she heard a voice, 'I thought you'd ran away, come back to bed.'

Ken stepped into the room and offered his hand and the two went back upstairs. He helped her off with the tee shirt.

Ken's cock was erect again and he positioned himself in front of Sharon and grabbed her knees, to pull her legs apart. Sharon looked up and pleaded, 'Ken, I'm sore.'

Ken leant across and opened a drawer in a bedside cabinet. He pulled out a tube of KY Jelly, took off the lid and squeezed some over the cock and rubbed it all over, in a masturbatory action, 'yes, Mary got sore as well, sometimes.'

Ken quickly grabbed Sharon's legs, pulled her onto his cock, put his arms around her back and they went into a roll, Sharon ending up straddled on top. He put both hands on her hips, moved her up and down on his cock, then let go, 'now you fuck me, baby and fuck me nice and hard, let's see those lovely tits bouncing.'

It was just getting light when Ken woke Sharon. He looked out of the window, then glanced over his shoulder, 'get dressed, we're leaving soon.' Ken was dressed in the clothes he'd worn yesterday. He opened a wardrobe and took out a shotgun, then reached up. took a box of cartridges and emptied it into his inside jacket pocket. He left the wardrobe door open and looked at Sharon, 'take Mary's clothes, it's alright, she was about the same size as you. There are trainers in the spare room. Take her walking ones, we're going through the fields and woods.'

Sharon put on a pair of charcoal adidas leggings and matching sweatshirt and she found a pair of Merrell walking trainers in the spare room, that fit her. She poured a bottle of water into the sink and quickly washed herself and tidied her hair, as best she could, then she went downstairs and into the close.

Ken was outside with the men, who were ready to leave.
One of the women wasn't happy, at all. It was the heavily pregnant woman. She had long brown hair, tied back and navy leggings, with a loose, cream maternity top, that draped over her bump. She was around thirty years old and quite attractive. Her face was bright red.
She walked over to the men, arms folded, then pointed at Sharon, 'so this is the reason you're all going to risk your lives. A new bike for you all to ride, you lonely fuckers.'

Some of the men, including Ken, put their heads down. They were obviously the single ones, who were living there.

She took one of the men's arm and raised her voice, 'look at me, Terry and you're going to fuck off and risk getting yourself killed? What do you think will happen to me and the baby if you don't come back?' She started to cry and Ken walked over and put his arm around her, 'Terry can stay here, Kathy.' Terry made to say something, but Ken cast him a look, which made him decide not to.

Ken addressed the group, 'Kathy has a good point, here, we never go out and leave the place unprotected. We need at least two men to stay here with Terry and the women.

We'll go ten strong to Bedlington.'

He looked around the group, 'Reg, Ade, you've both got young kids. Stay back. Make sure the women and kids are safe.' They both nodded and walked over to their wives.

Sharon looked around the houses. She could see young children peering out of the windows at her. She knew Mason and the others had guns, but she didn't want Ken to decide it was too dangerous, so she'd played this down, when they'd spoken about the Square, the night before, between fucks.

When the group left, there were birds everywhere the eye could see.

The noise of the constant cawing was deafening.

All ten men were carrying shotguns, but had iron bars, and crowbars tucked in their belts, to take out any dead they encountered, quietly. The guns were for the living.

Ken led the group to the road, just outside New Hartley, that leads to the Keel Row and they entered fields on the left side, 'we'll use the fields and head for Hartford Colliery.

We'll cross roads, where there aren't so many dead lying around. I'm not sure they're quite finished. We don't want any accidents.'

Sharon spoke up, 'some have taken wild animals, rabbits, foxes. There are groups walking on the main roads. I saw them.'

The group made their way to the outskirts of Hartford Colliery, then crossed fields and picked up a path that led to Humford woods. The walk was uneventful. There were no dead in the woods and they crossed the large concrete stepping stones and took some steep steps up into the parking area.

They sat on some picnic tables and Ken pointed into the woods, 'that path leads along to the Dam. About half way the path branches up and we can cross through a plantation and come out on the fields, above, that will take us over to the farm, at the bottom of Church Lane.

Sharon said they have people there, so we'll take that place first. If the two we're after are there, we off them and we're out of here, agreed? Just Clarke and Dawson die.' Everyone nodded and they all set off into the woods.

At the edge of the plantation, leading out onto the fields, Ken held up a hand. A pheasant was flapping about, at the edge of the field, then a pellet struck it and it fell dead. They heard a young boy's voice, 'don't worry, Daniel, you winged it, that's enough. It's still another one for the pot.'

The boy bent down to pick up the pheasant, before seeing any of the group and Ken stepped out of the woods, pointing the shotgun at him, 'put the gun down, son and you won't be hurt. You too, Daniel, is it?' Jamie Jones laid the air rifle against the fence and Daniel Miller dropped his by his feet.

Ken took both guns and checked they weren't loaded and passed them back to the boys. He held out his hand, 'pellets.' Jamie and Daniel emptied their pockets and Jamie opened a tin, poured the loose pellets inside and passed the tin to Ken.

Ken Knelt down in front of the kids, 'you're coming with us. I don't want you to lose your guns, so keep them, but they're not a weapon any more, today. I don't want either of you to get shot for pointing one of them at these men and they will shoot you, understand?' Jamie nodded.
Ken picked up a large sack, that contained dead rabbits and pheasants and he passed it to Daniel, 'you can still take these back. You'll be home soon.' Daniel swung the sack over his shoulder.

Sharon stepped forward and pointed at Jamie, 'I recognise this one, I saw him in Mason's window when the men were murdered.' Jamie looked at her, 'murdered? I saw you as well, that day, when my Grandad led you and the others out of the Square. No one was murdered, but we would have been, if Ray Donaldson had got what he wanted. Him and his friends attacked the Square. They were going to execute Grandad and the other men.'

Sharon stepped over and slapped Jamie's face and Ken pulled her aside. She turned and faced Jamie again, who was stood, head down, 'you're lying, we came to you for shelter and our men were murdered in cold blood. Kylie and Alec were murdered in cold blood, Ray, his brothers, my husband, Craig.'

Ken walked across and put his hand on Jamie's shoulder, 'I'm sorry that happened, son.' He glared at Sharon, 'it won't happen again.'

Jamie looked up, 'Alec's mum wasn't murdered, mister, she knows fine well. She's lied to you. Alec Donaldson…' He started to cry, 'Alec Donaldson raped my sister, Emma and killed her best friend, Kate. They killed Kate's whole family and left a baby for dead.' He looked at Sharon, 'you, you left baby Amalia for dead, all of you. Alec Donaldson was stalking us, obsessed with Emma and she…she hung herself.

She killed herself, rather than be taken by Alec Donaldson. She knows, don't you?' Sharon shook her head and looked away.

Ken addressed the group, 'the situation has changed. We're going to occupy Ray's house and the houses nearby. We'll send a message this afternoon to Mason, telling him we have these boys and offer an exchange, the boys for the two murderers.

They may resist, but they won't have the weapons, that we have.' He looked at Sharon, 'God help you if you've lying, Sharon. I know what Ray Donaldson was like. If you have anything to tell me, you better say it now.' Sharon looked Ken in the eyes, 'they murdered my husband, your sister and the others in cold blood. Clarke and Dawson deserve what they have coming.'

When they reached Millfield, Ken addressed the men, 'we need to clear some of the debris and bodies away from here, it's too messy. We'll drag the dead into the middle of the field, out of the way. Make Sure they're brain dead before picking them up, I've seen mouths opening and closing.'

Cynthia called for Amanda, from the bedroom, overlooking Millfield. Amanda walked into the room, 'what's up?' She looked out the window, between closed curtains.

There were people either side of the Millfield playing field. They went into houses, then they came back out, started hitting bodies across the head with bars and dragging them onto the field.

Cynthia grabbed Amanda's arm, 'they've got two boys. I saw them when they arrived. One of them is Don Mason's grandkid. They took them into Ray Donaldson's house. Sharon is with them. Oh God, what has she done?'

A few hours hour later, the men had cleared the road around Millfield and there was a large pile of bodies in the middle of the field. Cars had been pushed across all entrances into Millfiled, reinforcing the makeshift barriers that had been pushed aside by the massive horde of zombies, days earlier.

Ken walked over to one of the houses. He gave a note to one of the men, 'Benny, take this over to Hollymount Square, get their attention and pass this note on. Tell them it's for Don Mason.'

As he passed the note to Benny there was a deafening noise. The cawing bird sounds had turned to high pitched screeches and there were birds flying everywhere. He looked at Benny, 'what the fuck' and they both ran down to the main road.

Dead were still laid out, but lots of them were now eating birds. Injured crows and gulls were scrambling in all directions and being taken as they passed over bodies.

Ken turned back, 'forget the message, for now, Benny, we need to block these roads, properly.' Ken and Benny ran back to Millfield and alerted the rest of the men, most of whom had come outside to see what the noise was.

It was getting dark when Ken was satisfied the street was secure. There was dead walking around outside, but the group were adept at keeping out of sight and avoiding attention. They all locked down for the night, agreeing to meet at six am, all except Benny.

Benny was around twenty-five years old, five feet ten and very fit. He'd played football at a good level, before the outbreak and was very quick on his feet.

He had black hair and had grown a thick beard. He was wearing all charcoal coloured adidas, joggers, tee shirt and hoody, with samba trainers and looked as if he was just on his way out to football training.

Benny slipped out of Millfield and made is way alongside parked cars, down into Hollymount avenue. He took down two dead, that had wandered down the cobbled back road and he made his way to the 'cut,' or alley between Hollymount Square and Cornwall Crescent.

There was a wall between the houses, blocking the way in, but he could hear voices on the other side.

Benny took an empty glass bottle out of his hoody pocket, slipped the rolled up note inside, then threw it over the wall. He heard a voice say, 'what's that?' as the bottle smashed on the road, then someone ran towards the sound and stopped, 'it's a note.'

Benny slipped around the back of Hogarth Cottages, out onto Hollymount Avenue and, using the cover of abandoned cars, made his way safely back to Millfield.

Ken was looking out of Ray Donaldson's bedroom window when Benny scaled the barrier. Benny raised a thumb, then went inside the house across the way.

Millfield went silent.

11

The Meeting

Don arrived home at around eight - thirty pm. He'd asked Dawn and Clarky to go around the square and arrange the residents to meet at his house in half an hour.

Jean was sat in the dark. She'd helped herself to Don's whiskey and it hit her hard, so she had been in and out of sleep, but each time she woke, the realization kicked in about what had happened to her daughter and she'd broken down.

Don sat down beside her, 'I'm really sorry I left you the way I did, you shouldn't be on your own. It's just, my grandson…my grandson has been kidnapped.'

Don fought back tears and Jean put an arm around him, 'It's alright, Don. There's nothing you can do for Katie; you have to think about your own. I'm sorry, I wish there was something I could do.'

Don put his head down, 'I'm so sorry Jean, after what you've been through, being troubled with my problems. The men here at the Square, we'll get Jamie back.'

Don poured himself a drink and sat back in the settee. He put his hand on Jean's arm, 'listen, the residents of the square are coming over here. I'm just going to talk to them from the front door. I have a room for you upstairs. You don't have to…' 'I'm ok here, Don, I'd prefer your company for a while. I'll have another drink. If I'm asleep when you come back in, just leave me here.'

Don and Jean sat quiet. Both had experienced trauma no one should ever go through and now Don had the added worry of Jamie's kidnap.

His heart was racing with anxiety and his hands were shaking. Don knew events were taking their toll on him.

Jean soon nodded off again and Don took his coat from a hook by the front door and put it over her. It was nine o'clock and he could hear voices outside.

Don went to the front door and it went silent. He looked around the group. Some had brought paraffin lamps and put them down on the ground.

Don addressed the residents, 'You all know we were out today, trying to rescue our families and friends and I know a number of you have had tragic news. I'm deeply sorry for your loss, but we managed to find some survivors.

We lost one of our men, today, Connor Castle. Connor was bitten, while ensuring Hannah, myself and another survivor reached safety. He gave his life distracting the dead, to enable us to escape.

Connor was a very brave man and a man who ensured I would be safe on the Horton Road, that day, when he never even knew me.

Connor didn't suffer. I shot him dead, before the zombies converged on him. He'd asked me to do that for him.' Don put his head down and continued, 'I'm sorry, there will be no body to bury.' A tear ran down his face.

The residents were silent, as Don took a deep breath and continued, 'I've been told the kids have been sneaking out of the Farm and the Square, when the dead were lying down, but we need to get the word to all the kids, that the dead are back on their feet.

They have fed, you all heard the birds screaming, but this time their appetite seems insatiable. They are desperate for food and the most dangerous, I have seen them.

Two of our children have been kidnapped. The wife of one of Donaldson's friends, Sharon Thompson, has gone across to New Hartley and sought Kylie Donaldson's brother and he has brought a gang across to Millfield.

The man is called Ken Martin. He caught my grandson, Jamie and Daniel Miller, while they were shooting on the farm land. A letter was thrown into the square earlier.'

Ronnie Binns stepped forward and spoke, 'it sounds harsh, Don, but letting those women go could have cost us dearly, here.' Dawn Todd replied, 'I agree, Ronnie, but it would have been cold blooded murder, if we had killed them.

We did the right thing, letting them go. We weren't to know the dead would lie down. Sharon Thompson would never have made New Hartley if they hadn't.'

Eileen Moorehouse stepped forward and spoke, 'nevertheless, two of our kids are in danger, now. We need to get them back, what do they want in exchange for the boys? What's in the letter, Don?'

Don held up the letter, 'I'll read it out,'

'Mason, I am aware of the murder of my sister and her family, as well as a number of their friends. I know Ray Donaldson and his brothers were arseholes, so I expected them to eventually meet their match, in a world without law, but I am told my sister, her son and Craig Thompson were murdered in cold blood, trying to surrender to your people.

I cannot allow the perpetrators of this to go unpunished, so I offer you an exchange. The two boys for Ian Clarke and Paul Dawson.

If these two men come to Millfield at nine o'clock tomorrow morning, the two boys will be released. If the exchange is not made, I will shoot the two boys. Either way we will then be even and I will return to New Hartley.

If you attack my men tonight or any time tomorrow, the boys will die. Rest assured the boys will be safe with me for the night. All of my men are armed, but we have only come over here for two people.

You have the choice, which two people die.

Dowser stepped forward, 'no fucking way is my son going over there, Don. He murdered no one. Craig Thompson was armed and part of a gang that was here to kill you and Clarky. Paul defended this place.'

Clarky spoke up, 'I didn't kill Kylie Donaldson, Don. You saw her body. She had been bit. Alec Donaldson offed her. I did kill the serial child rapist murderer, though, I'll give them that.' 'I killed him, Clarky.' Marty Pickering stepped forward. 'If they want revenge for Alec Donaldson, it's me they want.'

Clarky glanced at Marty, 'not it isn't. Just shut up Marty, you've been through enough. I'll go in exchange for the boys. I'll take responsibility for it all. Don told me the fire was a bad idea and I knew the feud with Ray Donaldson would come around and bite my arse one day. I'll go.'

Eileen Moorehouse replied, 'no you won't, Ian. Just quit the fucking bravado for a minute. If they think we'll just hand over people to be executed, where will it stop?

What if they're short of food, or need equipment, weapons, women? Do we just hand it over if they promise to go away?

I'm sorry, Don, but I've arrested enough arseholes in my time to know that if people who would go as far as kidnapping kids, see weakness, they'll be back, over and over again.

I know they have the boys, but I'm one hundred percent that this is just the start.

They need to be scared to come back here, Don, shit scared, and you fucking know this fine well, Ian, so cut the bullshit and come up with a solution that isn't a surrender.

Does anyone here think they would have been still alive if you had surrendered to Ray fucking Donaldson, Don?' She looked around, 'I thought not.'

There was whispering between people and Midgy spoke next, 'how many guns do we have, now, Don? Vic brought back rifles, this afternoon and tonight.

We've got a shotgun, revolvers. I say we all go there. What if this cunt kills the kids anyway? Donaldson would have. I say arm as many men as possible and walk over.

Offer them an exchange of our own. Any harm comes to the boys and they all die.'

Paul Dawson spoke, 'Dad, I know you're upset, but the first priority is to get the boys back. Even if we kill them all, we've failed if our boys are harmed. I should go with Clarky.

Whatever we're going to do has to be done after the boys get out.

I did cut that wanker's head off and I'd do it again, if it means you, mam and Marie are safe from those fuckers.'

Don looked around the group. He could see everyone was scared. He was terrified, himself. They had been through hell; some just being told today about lost relatives. Don nodded towards Vic, 'what about you, Vic. What do you think?'

Clarky shook his head and sighed, 'aye, Johnny Fucking Rambo. How are you going to bring a world of shit down this time, on a gang that's holding two of our children?'

Vic stepped forward, 'I'm not, Clarky. I see it as there are two ways out of this. We give you and Paul up, they shoot you both in the back of the heads and, hopefully leave, or, tomorrow morning you all do exactly what I tell you here.'

Vic looked around. The residents were silent. Vic looked Don's way, 'Don?' Don nodded, then spoke, 'listen, let's hear Vic out. He rescued two Nedderton boys from four men this evening, at the golf course.

These men were a big threat to us and they were very dangerous. If anyone can do it, it's Vic.'

Clarky smiled and shook his head, 'howay then, Action Man, Paul and me end up dead in plan 'a' so you've got two on your side, before you even speak about plan 'b.' Eileen stepped closer to Clarky and linked arms.

Vic stood on the short wall, outside Don's house, 'right, this is how it goes down, then...'

12

Safe for the Night

Ken had allowed the two boys to clean the rabbits and pheasants, they had shot. They sat, in candlelight, locked in the wash house, Jamie gutting and skinning rabbits and Daniel plucking pheasants, as Ken met with the men in Donaldson's kitchen.

Ken addressed the group, 'we are only here for the two murderers, so let's only start shooting, if necessary. It's likely they'll exchange the two men for the boys, when they see our guns.

Sharon has seen their defences and they survive, mainly with clubs and spikes. We have them outgunned, so we all meet out there at quarter to nine. Get this done and we go back home.

Benny, you come over here, when they appear. You stay with the boys and I'll call you out to do the exchange.' Benny nodded.

Ken glanced at Sharon and then back at the men, 'ok, let's go dark and quiet until morning.' The men all left.

The two boys were brought back in, as Jamie had just started to tidy up and hang the game.

Ken led them back into the sitting room, 'leave it until morning, it's too late and I don't want light showing at this time of night. We go dark and quiet.'

They sat silent until around eleven o'clock, then Ken led the boys upstairs. He opened the door of the room, overlooking the rear garden and led them inside.

Ken knelt beside the boys, as they sat on the bed, 'I'm not locking doors, or anything, but I will tell you, if you try to get away you will be shot. You can use the upstairs toilet, but, otherwise do not leave this room. You will be returned to your folks tomorrow, I promise, but you need to comply, here. I really don't want to hurt either of you.'

Around one am Jamie woke up with a start. Sharon Thomson was stood over the bed, holding a large kitchen knife. She'd closed the door behind her.

Jamie held a hand over Daniel's mouth as he woke and the two sat up. Daniel was terrified and began to cry and Jamie put an arm on his shoulder, 'it's alright, Daniel, she won't hurt us. She knows their leader needs us alive.'

Sharon pointed the knife towards them, 'I will fucking hurt the two of you, mark my words, if either of you tell any more of your lies about what happened to my Craig. Paul Dawson murdered him, you saw it and you fucking lied to Ken, making me look like a liar. I'll fucking cut your throat if it happens again.'

Jamie shook his head, 'you know the truth. My grandad spared you and the others. He gave you a chance to survive and look what you have done. Your husband was armed and dangerous and with a gang that had invaded our home with the intention to murder people.

He was part of Donaldson's gang, that were beating innocent survivors to death with baseball bats, every day. No, Daniel, she won't use that knife. She knows harming us would be more than her life is worth. If Ken doesn't kill her for it, my grandad will.'

Sharon walked to the bedroom door and turned back, 'you've been warned.' She slipped out of the room and crossed the landing back into the main bedroom.

Daniel was still shaking and Jamie put an arm around him, 'just ignore her, mate. The leader of the group, Ken. He told them all we are not to be harmed. If we just do as he says, we'll be back home tomorrow. Grandad will come up with something. He won't let them hurt anyone.'

Jamie couldn't sleep and an hour later got up and looked out of the window. It was dark outside, but he could make out the fence along the bottom of the garden, in front of the Millfield South bungalows.

He saw something move and tried to focus, then a man stepped out from behind the fence. He was just illuminated enough by the moonlight to enable Jamie to recognise him. It was Vic Hind.

Jamie immediately held up a hand and Vic did the same. Vic gave a thumbs up, with a puzzled look and Jamie nodded and gave a thumbs up back.

Vic held his arms out then one after the other, made a counting gesture, with his fingers. Jamie held up both hands, palms out. Vic held out his fists and one at a time raised a finger until all ten showed. Jamie nodded.

Vic held out his arms again then gestured, as if shooting a gun. Again, Jamie held up ten fingers and Vic confirmed.

Vic held up his hands in the shape of a house, then again gestured for numbers. Jamie held up one hand and Vic confirmed five. Jamie pointed down, left, right, back left and right.

Vic pointed to the back wash house door, then made a gesture, as if unlocking a door. Jamie nodded.

Vic held a thumbs up again. He cupped two hands together and put them on the side of his head and Jamie nodded. He turned to Daniel, who had gone back to sleep, then looked over to where he'd seen Vic. Vic was gone.

Jamie went back to bed. He thought about Vic's visit and felt comforted that something was going on that may prevent Clarky and Paul coming to harm. He'd decided to say nothing to Daniel about seeing Vic.

Around seven am. Ken led Jamie and Daniel downstairs. He had found some snickers bars in a bedroom drawer and he gave the boys one each, with some lemonade, from a bottle that had been left in the fridge.

Jamie finished his snickers bar and asked Ken if he could finish off in the wash house. Ken nodded and Jamie left the kitchen, leaving the door open and took down rabbits and birds he'd tied up and hung from a nail the ceiling rafter.

He put them all into a sack, then took the bag of guts and skins to the back wash house door, opened the door and dropped the tied up plastic bag into the wheelie bin. When he returned, he pretended to lock the door, rattling the key a bit, then returned to the kitchen.

Ken was sat beside Sharon at the kitchen table and Daniel had gone into the sitting room.

As Jamie went to join him Ken looked up, 'nine o'clock, we'll be exchanging you for the two murderers. Go back to the bedroom. Stay there. Benny will be in the house, so don't leave the bedroom until he tells you.

I warn you Jamie, Daniel, if you try anything, I'll shoot a lot more of them.'
Jamie nodded and walked through to the sitting room. He passed Daniel on the way to the stairs, patting his shoulder on the way past, 'we have to go back to the room, Daniel. He'll tell us when we have to go.'

Daniel got up and the two boys made their way back to the bedroom.

13

The Exchange

Don and Jean both woke with a start. They were sat, huddled together on the settee and Don quickly got to his feet, 'I, I'm sorry, I must have…' Jean smiled, 'it's ok, Don. Thank you for not leaving me on my own.'

Don started up a small butane gas camping stove and put the kettle on, that he'd topped up with bottled water. He looked over, as Jean was hanging his coat back up, 'I can make us some toast,' 'toast, how?'

Don went into a bread bin in the kitchen and held up an un cut loaf, 'the girls bake. We get bread, cake, scones. I use my blowtorch to toast it.' 'Jean smiled, 'toast would be lovely.' Don cut four slices of bread.

Don had a gas bottle in the corner of the kitchen and took a blowtorch, that was connected, lit it and charred the bread, he'd just sliced and laid on a baking tray.

He took a jar of peanut butter and a jar of Nutella out of the cupboard and the two sat together in the kitchen having tea and toast.

Jean was subdued and very quiet. The magnitude of what she'd witnessed the day before was still sinking in and she felt waves of emotions, almost reducing her to tears, throughout.

Don noticed her distress and topped up her tea, 'you never get over something like this, Jean. I lost my granddaughter, not long back. It was like my whole world had fallen in, but I convinced myself that my grandson and the people here, need me and that gets me by.
Your husband?' Jean put her head down, 'I don't know, Don. He called me when things were getting bad. Said he would call every hour, but I never heard from him again.

I know the roads were blocked in every direction and he was stuck on a motorway. I know he was scared. I just hope he found a way out, but I know the motorways and roads were overrun, everywhere.

He said was trying to stay in his cab, because fights were breaking out on the roadsides, but how long could he stay in a lorry cab, in a traffic jam, as far as the eye could see?'

Don took Jean's hand, 'if you want, I can arrange a house for you, this morning, before we go out.' Jean held his hand in return, 'if it's alright with you, I'd prefer to stay here, you mentioned a spare room?' Don nodded, 'of course, Jean.' Jean looked Don in the eyes, 'thank you, Don. Thank you for what you did for me out there.' Don smiled, 'it's ok, Jean, stay here as long as you like.'

Jamie and Daniel were sat on the bed in Alec Donaldson's room. Daniel was terrified. He knew at nine o'clock they would be sent out among the men with guns and that they could get shot if it went wrong. Jamie was scared too, but tried not to show it.

Ken had reassured the two boys that he intended no harm to come to them, before ordering them back to the bedroom and the two boys sat quiet until they heard voices downstairs.

It was eight fifty am and Paul Dawson and Ian Clarke had been seen adjacent to the flats at Millfield East, standing on their own, around forty yards down the road.

Benny was at the Donaldson house front door and Ken told him to stay inside and bring the boys out on his call.

Ken and Sharon walked across to the entrance of Millfield. Three men, armed with shotguns joined them from the house next door and, across the other side of Millfield, five armed men were standing on the footpath.

They all walked over to the blockade of cars and watched as Ian Clark stepped forward, 'you called for an exchange, the two of us for the boys. We're here, now. Tell me how this is going to go.'

Ken stepped forward.

The back door of Ray Donaldson's wash house silently opened and closed. Benny was inside the house, watching out of the living room window, waiting for the call from Ken. He was holding a twelve bore shotgun, but quickly dropped it to the floor, when he felt the knife against his throat.

Vic kicked the gun to the side, 'I have no intention of killing you, son, just do as I say. I have a silenced revolver and if you so much as fucking blink the wrong way, I'll put a hole in you, understand.' Benny nodded. He was so scared he couldn't talk.

Vic walked Benny to the door, knife still to his throat and whispered, 'open the door, sunshine, step out and close it behind you, then walk slowly over to the others.'

Benny walked out of the front garden and slowly walked towards Ken and the gang. He called out, 'Ken, Ken, there's a man in the house, he's armed.'

Ken turned and looked at the house. Vic was now in the front bedroom window and he waved. Ken raised the shotgun and fired both barrels, blowing out the window.

Shattered glass rained against the back wall of the bedroom and Vic spun round, from the side and aimed the rifle at Ken from the window.

The other men began to raise their guns and Vic called out, 'If one gun goes off here, your leader dies. This is an automatic weapon and I can take most of you down, please don't make me do it.'

Ken had fired both barrels of the shotgun and he dropped it to the floor. He looked up at Vic, and said, 'the same goes for you, mate, you fire and you're dead, just look at what one gun did to the window.'

Ken glanced over his shoulder, 'If he shoots, fire both barrels at the window, all of you.'

'I wouldn't.' Clarky was standing twenty feet away holding a revolver, two handed. Paul was alongside him holding another. Behind them were Midgy, Dowser, Don, Hannah, Eileen, Chris Dewhirst and Ronnie, all armed.

Benny grabbed Ken's arm, 'look.' Geordie Wells was walking down from the Church lane end of Millfield with Will and ten of the farm kids. Geordie was carrying his shotgun and the kids all had catapults.

Don Mason stepped forward, 'I believe your name is Ken Martin.' Ken looked across at Don, 'I'm Kylie Donaldson's brother, you know Kylie, one of the people your tribe fucking murdered.'

Don took another few steps forward, 'we can talk about this, son, but not with guns pointing. Put the weapons down and we can straighten this out.

I'll take my grandson back and you and these lads leave here safely. Come on now, Ken. The gunshot will have attracted dead. Put the guns down and let us in. Let's sort this out.'

Ken shook his head, 'keep the fucking guns on them, this is what they did to Ray and his brothers, Craig, isn't it Sharon?

They fucking murdered them when they put their weapons down. Ken was now very agitated and the panic was spreading among the others.

Vic steadied is aim from the window. He didn't like how this was going. Don was a goner, if one of those guns went off.

It was silent for a few moments, people either side of the divide aiming guns at each other. Don had realised he couldn't gain Ken's trust and stepped back, 'so be it, Ken. If any of you make to fire on us, you will all be shot.

This is not what I came here for, but you kidnapped my grandkid. I've done everything I can possibly do to reason with you.'

All of Ken's men were looking at each other, terrified. Benny pleaded with Ken, 'there's too many guns, Ken, we haven't got a chance,' Ken spat back, 'we've got a better chance than without them Benny, you heard what they did to Ray and the others.'

There was a loud voice from behind Ken's men, 'I can help here, gentlemen.' A white-haired man walked down from Millfield North, climbed over the bonnet of a car and walked right among the armed New Hartley men. It was Ed from Nedderton.

He stood beside Ken and looked around, 'seems like you've got yourself and these lads into a bit of a pickle, son.' Ken shook his head, 'who the fuck are you and what the fuck are you doing walking among men armed with fucking shotguns, are you fucking mad?'

Ed shook his head, 'no, son, just older and wiser than you. You've got no reason to shoot me and if you do shoot me, the men in Millfield North, over there will fucking skin you all alive and feed you to my pigs.'

Ken looked over. There was a group of men standing, all holding shotguns. Eustace waved up to Vic in the window and Vic shook his head and headbutted the window sill, with a huge grin, 'for fuck's sake.'

Ed picked up Ken's gun and looked at the other men, 'two of our children were kidnapped, by armed men. These people rescued them.

They were looking for their own boys, that I believe you had kidnapped, around the same time. I don't believe these people would murder anyone in cold blood. This man here,' he pointed at Don, 'wishes to discuss this with you and you are on the point of a shootout, because you don't trust him. So, let me be the mediator.

Put the guns down, both sides and come over here and talk.' Benny looked at Ken, 'Ken, I think we should…' Ken held out his arm, 'lay down the guns.'

Ed stood and looked around the group of New Hartley men, 'The dead here are after all of us. Life is hard enough, without having the added problems of kidnapping innocent children. It has to stop.

Now we know the other kidnappers won't do it again, they ended up eaten, but we need an outcome, here that returns these boys, safely home, with no more killing and I mean no more killing, not one.'

The guns were laid on the bonnet of one of the cars in the blockade and Don, Clarky, Paul and Dowser, scaled the barrier.

Four dead had appeared from the front street and Chris, Ronnie and Hannah walked towards them, having exchanged their guns for clubs.

Don stood before Ken and the others, 'I don't know what you have been told, son, but Donaldson and his men were terrorising Bedlington.' Will Masters and Geordie arrived and Geordie handed his gun to Ed. The farm kids stayed well back.

Geordie put his hand on Will's shoulder, 'this boy has been searching Bedlington for child survivors, since he lost his parents. You know why, mate? He'd been rescuing children to prevent Alec Donaldson from raping and murdering them. If you don't believe me, come over to the farm. It's an orphanage. Ask the kids what they feared most. It won't be fucking zombies.'

Will spoke, 'The Donaldsons murdered the Ashford family over there. They did it because they reported a rape to the police, that happened in their home, before all this. Emma Jones, Don's granddaughter was the victim. She later took her own life because the same monster was stalking her. It was Alec Donaldson. He even took Emma's friend, Kate into the park, under Emma's window and cut her throat, as Emma watched on, helplessly.

When they murdered the Ashfords, they left a baby in the house. A helpless baby left on her own and Alec Donaldson had killed her mother and left her in the open doorway. If she'd turned, she would have eaten her own baby. The child is in Hollymount Square, now. I could tell you of dozens of murders, where I'd got to friends of mine, too late. He was terrorising Bedlington.'

Clarky was next to speak, 'I killed Ray Donaldson.' He looked at the large, scorched patch on the field, across the way, 'I'm not going to dispute it. I fucking hated the man and I killed the spineless cunt. So, yes, your right. I did for Ray and fucking Alec Donaldson, oh and Sammy fucking Dodds, as well, but what Sharon fucking Thompson, the Millfield oracle of information, here might not have told you,' he glared at Sharon, 'was that Donaldson, his son, brothers, her fucking coward husband, Craig, Sammy fucking Dodds, Gary Fucking Blewitt, the fucking 'a' team, stabbed my wife and left her to bleed out, down Dene View.

Now, that was cold blooded murder, Ken, unprovoked. All she did was open the door, thinking it was me.

They did it for no reason. She had no differences with them. They did it because they were arseholes. Looting houses, murdering terrified survivors, for money they couldn't fucking spend and alcohol, they had gallons of.

They murdered an old woman, the same day at Dene View, took her in a back garden and beat her head to a pulp. They got a few tins of beans and hot dogs from her kitchen, that I had just left for her and a twenty pound note out of her purse.

They killed a helpless old woman for nothing. She would have given them her last if they had told her they were hungry.

You've come here to avenge your sister. Alec Donaldson killed your sister, mate. Not only did he kill her, but he cut off her head. You'll find the body in one of the houses on the Horton road. That's where she got bit.

I don't know what he did with the head, but he was a very, very disturbed fucker. Maybe he had a head funeral, or he cut it off because he couldn't carry her whole body, maybe we'll never know?'

Don spoke, 'Ken, if you do find Kylie's body, check her leg. Vic and I found her. I saw the bite.

Clarky is telling you the truth, as he'd heard it from me. He wasn't there, at Horton Road, it was me.' Don gave a knowing glance to Clarky.

Sharon lunged towards the guns and grabbed a shotgun, turning towards Paul Dawson. It was cocked and ready to fire. Vic took aim, from the window, but didn't have a clear shot through the crowd.

Sharon screamed at Ken, 'don't believe any of this, Ken, it was cold blooded murder, he killed my Craig.' Sharon aimed the gun at Paul and fired, just as she was tackled to the ground. Both barrels were discharged into the air. Amanda Blewitt threw the gun aside and punched Sharon three times in the face. She got to her feet holding Sharon's hair and repeatedly kicked her in the chest and lower body, until Benny grabbed her and pulled her back.

Sharon tried to get to her feet and Amanda broke free from Benny and punched her in the mouth, knocking out two teeth. Sharon went down again and Amanda kicked her in the lower body, one more time, 'fucking cunt! Leaving our front door wide open and fucking off to New Hartley. We could have been eaten in our own bed, you fucking idiot. What did we do to deserve that, you twisted cow? Bring the camera over, Cyn'

Cynthia stepped forward.

Amanda and Cynthia had seen the commotion out of the window and made their way around the footpath, unnoticed. Cynthia was carrying the video recorder from Alec Donaldson's rape room.

Amanda took the camera and handed it to Ken, 'press play.' Ken stood in tears as the footage played of Alec Donaldson raping, then murdering a young girl. He said nothing, as he passed the camera back to Amanda.

Cynthia walked over and put a hand on Ken's shoulder, 'we were there, Ken. Kylie wasn't murdered. She ran away with Alec. They were heading for your place.

I believe Kylie was bit. Don Mason caught up with Alec and brought him back. If anyone, Mason would have killed Alec, not Kylie.

It's true, Ken Alec had raped Don's granddaughter, before the outbreak. He was in custody when the pandemic started. They released him to house arrest when it was getting out of control, then he…then the murders and rapes started. There are more tapes, Ken.

The men were killed in Hollymount Square in a failed attempt to murder Ian Clarke and Don Mason. They wanted to take over Hollymount Square, because it was safe and secure. It was all Ray Donaldson's doing. These people just defended themselves.'

Ken stood, silent. He looked at Sharon, who had just got back to her feet. Her nose and mouth were bleeding and she was sobbing. He looked at Clarky, 'let us have our guns and we'll go. We have families at New Hartley and need the weapons to defend ourselves.'

Clarky nodded.

Eileen Moorehouse walked over and spoke to Ken from behind the barrier, 'rest assured that our community is heavily armed and strong in defence.' She looked at Ed, 'the way I see it is that this man saved all of your lives and you should be grateful to him, but if we see any of you in these parts again, we will not only shoot you, but we will head straight for New Hartley and eliminate the whole threat. We know where you live, Maple Court. Don't ever come back here.'

Ken nodded and the men picked up their weapons, breaking the barrels, to carry them. He looked up to the bedroom window. Vic still had the gun on him. He nodded to Vic and Vic walked away from the window and came downstairs to the front door.

Vic walked over and passed the shotgun to Benny and said, 'take care, son,' Benny nodded and took the gun. Vic had a blanket and bin liner in the other hand and walked over to the pile of dead as the men left.

Don and the group stood together as Ken and his men walked down Millfield East, and along a path that led to the top of the picnic field and the short cut towards Humford. Sharon was trailing behind them.

Don shook Ed's hand, 'thanks, Ed, that could have got ugly.' Ed smiled, 'The lad, Ken had no intention of firing, when he saw you were armed. He just wanted them all safely out and that's what he got.'

Jamie and Daniel ran across the field and they both hugged Don, then Daniel ran to Geordie. Geordie took him in his arms. They were both crying. Geordie looked in the boy's eyes and said, 'thank God you're alright, son.'

Vic made his way over with the bin liner, by his side, containing the rolled-up blanket. He passed it to Ed, 'present for you, Ed, in gratitude for your help.'

Ed opened the bag, then quickly tied it again, 'is this some sort of joke, Vic.' Vic was laughing and shook his head, 'not at all, Ed. The blanket in that bag is covered in zombie slime, their shit, if you like. Cover up with that blanket and you can walk among them.

They recognise sound, smell and sight. Interrupt the senses and they're not interested in you.'

Ed passed the bag to Eustace, 'this could be a game changer for us, now the dead are walking again, Vic, thank you very much.' 'my pleasure, Ed, just remember, equal parts water and slime makes the paint, it doesn't need to be that strong.'

Don accompanied Ed back to his men, 'Maybe, Ed, we could work together in some way? Perhaps trade stuff?' He passed Ed his walkie. We stay on channel seven. Maybe we could just chat before committing to anything?' Ed smiled, 'I'll be in touch, Don, but now, just get your people home safely.'

Don walked back to Amanda and Cynthia and shook both their hands, 'it was big of you both to do what you did, thank you. I'm going to speak with the residents. Suggest you return, if you want to?' They both nodded.

Amanda and Cynthia watched as Don and the others returned to the front street and out of view. They turned, linked arms and slowly made their way back to the house, Amanda still carrying the video camera.

Cynthia pulled Amanda close, 'do you think they'll let us back in?' Amanda stopped and looked back, 'well Ken and his goons have blocked the entrances, here and we still have heaps of food and drink, so let's wait and see.

I think the two of us are ok in the meantime. Fancy a drink? The residents here, before were wine drinkers. There's a full rack in the wash house. Red, white, sparkling Cava.' Cynthia smiled, 'I'd love a glass and Cava sounds good.'

Where Next for Sharon?

The New Hartley men were half way across the field, towards Humford, when Ken stopped and turned around, 'where the fuck do you think you're going?' Sharon was ten yards behind.

She stopped and held out her hands, 'Ken, please, I can't go back, there. I want to be with you.'

Ken walked over and slapped Sharon's face so hard it took her off her feet and she took a few moments to regain her senses, then she looked up at him. Ken was stood over her holding a hunting knife, 'you fucking liar. We risked our lives, coming over here, just so you could get revenge on a bloke who offed your husband in self - defence.

You fucking lied about my sister's fucking death and you think I'll take you back with me and play happy families?'

Ken looked around the men, then back at Sharon, 'some of these men have kids. Every time we leave the Close it's a risk, but you, you put us in front of guns. You fucking knew they were armed, but all you wanted was the Dawson bloke dead, never mind anyone else.

No, fuck off back to Bedlington you twisted cunt. If you're still behind us, when we get to the path to Humford, I'll cut your fucking throat.'

Sharon heard one of the men in the group mutter, 'cut the fucker now.' She stood up, quickly turned and headed back towards Millfield South.

When Sharon reached the edge of the field, she looked back. Ken and the men were just going out of sight. She turned and made her way back towards Millfield.

As the men reached Humford and crossed the stepping stones, Benny made for the track up bank that led up to the shortcut towards the Horton Road.

The others followed and Ken called out, 'this way, guys.' Benny stopped and turned around, 'But, Ken, your sister's body?'

Ken made his way alongside the Burn that led towards Hartford Colliery and called back, 'too risky. I've put you all in enough danger for one day, come on, we're going home.'

When she reached the flats on Millfield East, Sharon stopped and pulled back behind a gable end. Four dead were passing and they slowly made their way along Millfield South, occasionally stopping and tipping their heads to the side, on the alert for anything living.

When the dead were half way along the road, Sharon walked out and up to the end of the front block of flats.

She looked towards the Front Street. She could see a number of zombies, wandering aimlessly, but she knew there was nothing for her in that direction. She turned and headed for the barrier across the entrance to Millfield and climbed over.

'You won't believe this, Amanda.' Cynthia was at the bedroom window and Amanda joined her, put her glass of Cava on the windowsill and they watched Sharon approach the house.

They went downstairs and Amanda picked up the video camera, quickly ejecting the tape. Then she went into her handbag. Cynthia walked into the sitting room and stood beside her, 'what are you doing, Amanda?' Amanda looked up, 'you'll see.'

There was a knock at the door and Amanda answered. Sharon was standing crying, 'I have nowhere to go. I've come back here.' She made to enter the house and Amanda pushed her hard with both hands.

Sharon fell to the ground, outside and Amanda stood over her, 'no fucking way are you getting back in here. You fucking left the door wide open when you ran away. It was no accident.

You wanted the dead to get in here, but they didn't, thank God. No, Sharon, you're a liability.

Don Mason is going to ask the residents of Hollymount to take us back in. We have no chance of this, if you're here, with your fucking morbid obsession with Paul Dawson.'

Sharon looked up, 'I don't care what you say, what Mason said, or any of the others. Craig was innocent. He did nothing wrong. He was murdered, murdered in cold blood.'

Amanda took a breath to compose herself. She was so angry, she was shaking and could hardly talk, 'nothing wrong, Sharon, Saint Craig did nothing wrong?' She held out her hand and Cynthia passed her the video camera. Amanda pressed play, passed the camera to Sharon then turned and faced Cynthia, 'I'm sorry I lied to you Cyn. It was all the men, Gary, as well. I tried to keep it from her and shut it out, myself, but I can't anymore.'

Cynthia took Amanda in her arms, as she broke down crying.

Sharon looked down at the camera screen. A terrified, naked young teenage girl was tied to the bed and Sharon heard a familiar voice, 'are you scared, little girl? You should be.' She had a look of absolute horror, as she watched her husband, Craig enter the shot, naked and position himself between the legs of the naked child. Sharon dropped the camera on the ground and began screaming, hysterically. It was like her world had just fallen in.

Amanda slapped Sharon's face and grabbed her by the hair, 'we're going back inside and, if we see you again, we'll kill you. Go, Sharon. You're not welcome anywhere around here. Millfield is ours and we'll soon be going around all these houses, one by one. If you're in one of them you're fucking dead.'

Sharon walked back into Millfield and made her way to the barrier over the entrance to Church lane. She climbed over and walked through onto Church lane.

The four dead she had seen making their way along Millfield South had just passed and headed along Church Lane, but had turned back, when they'd heard her screams. They had seen Sharon scale the barrier, so she turned left and ran away from them, in the other direction, along towards Millfield South.

Sharon went from door to door, desperately trying to get into the houses. After each locked door, the dead were closing in on her. As she got half way along the row of bungalows, Sharon got to an open door and she scrambled inside, desperately trying to close the door behind her.

The keep for the door latch and mortice locks had been busted off the frame, where someone had forced the door to break in.

If Sharon had gone through and out the open back door, she'd have found the residents, an old couple, lying face down in the garden, heads caved in by Ray Donaldson's baseball bat, some time back, but she focussed everything on getting the front door closed.

The dead were within a few feet of the front door, when Sharon grabbed at the security chain and she pushed the door closed again, desperately fumbling on the chain and it went into the slot, just as the dead got there.

The four dead bumped against the door, but it held shut. Sharon put her head against the side wall and cried. She was trembling with fear and took deep breaths, to try and compose herself. She put her hand to her mouth. Her lip was still bleeding and she felt the gap, where, she'd lost teeth. She spat blood onto the carpet and glanced again back at the door, that the four dead were bumping against.

As Sharon pulled herself together, she turned to make her way into the sitting room and immediately screamed with terror.

A young girl was standing in front of her. The girl had long, blonde hair and was wearing dirty leggings, white trainers and a yellow puffer jacket, zipped up. She had no bites, but Sharon could see major bruising on her throat.

The girl dropped black wings and legs, that seemed just held together by a length of tendon.

It was all that was left of a black bird she'd fed on hours earlier and the girl walked towards Sharon, reaching out with her arms.

Sharon was cornered in the small entrance hallway at the front door and she tried to push the girl aside to get past, but the girl grabbed her and held tight, her cold hands, almost going through the flesh on Sharon's arms. Sharon desperately tried to fight the girl off, but they both fell to the ground and Sharon felt excruciating pain, as the girl bit into her side, just under her left armpit.

Sharon was screaming and she instinctively grabbed at the injury, which was bleeding heavily. The girl still had a tight hold on her and chewed and swallowed the flesh she'd bitten off, spitting out a blood-soaked bit of cotton that had torn off Sharon's top.

Sharon was screaming for help, but there were only dead outside and, as the girl bit again, this time biting a chunk out of Sharon's left breast, the security chain on the door gave and the four zombies stumbled into the bungalow.

The girl sat up, contentedly chewing the second mouthful of food, she'd just taken and the four hungry dead converged on Sharon. The screams were deafening, as Sharon was bit on the face, chest, right arm and thigh, all at once and she was still conscious, as two of the group took their second bite, this time from her neck and left arm.

Sharon sat up. It was dark all around. She looked around, but there was nothing. Others like her were sat around her. Sharon stood up. She had a pain and she knew she needed something. She needed something to make the pain go away.

Sharon clumsily hobbled out into the dark, tripping over the thresh of the open door and fell flat on her face. She stood back up and started walking again.

The others like her stood up and followed her. Sharon stopped, looked around and turned her head to the side. She heard nothing. She sniffed, nothing. She looked around again.

Sharon began walking. She would walk until she found something. Something to alleviate this terrible feeling in her stomach.

15

Missing Persons

The Hollymount Square group were jubilant, as they headed back to the square. Not because they had gained some sort of victory, but because the kids were safe and no one was harmed.

Hannah, Chris, Paul and Midgy led the way, caving in skulls of a few dead who were attracted their way and they stood guard as the others entered the Square through the metal gate.

Don walked alongside Clarky and Eileen and, as they got to Clarky's house, Don took his arm and looked him in the eyes, 'Kylie Donaldson's head? Her body was intact when I left that house, Clarky. What the fuck were you on about, there?' Clarky smiled, 'you got me again, Don. I thought I'd got away with it as well.'

Don followed him to the door and took his arm again, 'got away with what, Clarky?'

Clarky opened the door, Eileen passed into the house and Clarky walked back up the garden path and sat on the wall. Don sat beside him.

Clarky was in thought for a few moments, then looked at Don and said, 'what I did to Donaldson was calculated and thought through in every detail, Don and I'd have taken a bullet, today for what I'd done, without hesitation. Maeve was everything to me, everything in the world and those fuckers took her away.

Sammy Dodds and Abe Gardener begged for mercy after I shot them. Ray had run away, abandoned them and I sat inside the house listening to them being eaten alive. It wasn't enough, though.

I sat for hours with Maeve, at home, trying to summon up the courage to blow my brains out, then you arrived.

I wasn't ok, Don and I'm not now. When I had Donaldson, I wanted him to go through horror, like I did, more even. Yes, I went over to the Horton Road and took Kylie Donaldson's head.'

Don gasped and Clarky put out his arms, 'what? Do you think I could carry that spit roast whore's body all that way back here? No fucking way.

I took her head and bagged it. It was hidden inside the fire and, when I went in there Marty wanted to kill the son, in revenge for his sister, so I let him. What was I thinking, Don? letting a kid knife someone.

When Marty left, I put the head in Ray's lap. I thought it was fitting that Kylie Donaldson's head was in a man's lap right till the end, don't you?'

Don didn't even smile, 'you cut the ties off Alec Donaldson when he'd died, so Ray would be eaten by his own son. Fucking hell, Clarky,'

Clarky nodded, 'eaten by his own son, while being burned alive and sucked off by his delightful wife, Spit Roast's severed head, to be exact.' Don couldn't make out whether Clarky was laughing or crying.

Clarky put a hand on Don's shoulder, 'Don, I know you didn't want things to go the way they did and I am sorry. I'm sorry the boys were put in danger. It's all my fault, but it couldn't continue with Ray and Alec Donaldson alive.

I did what I did to keep their deaths from the conscience of everyone here. There had been enough killing and you know this. You turned people away, rather than shoot them and, having her life spared wasn't enough for one of them.

Sharon Thompson brought even more trouble to our door and she will again, if she gets the chance.'

Don stood up and made off towards home. Jamie had run on ahead, carrying the bag of rabbits and pheasants. Don turned and looked at Clarky, 'all this is over now, Clarky. Our enemies are the dead and they're back on their feet. Your fight is over. Or is it just starting, mate?' Don walked off. Clarky sat for a few more minutes on the wall. Tears ran down his face and he put his hands on his head.

Clarky was sobbing, when Eileen walked down the garden path and put a hand on his shoulder, 'are you alright, Ian.' Clarky looked up, 'no, I'm not, Eileen.' Eileen took Clarky's hand and led him inside the house, closing the door behind them.

Jamie went straight to his room, when he got inside the house. Chris Dewhirst had left the air rifles at the front door and Jamie knew he was in trouble for leaving the square, so took them and put them away safe.

Don entered the front room and called on Jamie, who came to the top of the stairs. Don looked up, 'we have a guest, Jamie, she's called Jean, have you seen her?' Jamie called back down, as he stepped back towards the bedroom, 'she's not up here, Grandad.'

Don checked the back garden and wash house, then went out into the square. He made his way over to the central gardens and walked around.

A few of the kids were weeding the vegetable gardens and he about turned and headed back into the Square. Don made his way, door to door along all the occupied houses. No one had seen Jean.

Vic appeared at the top of the square. He was doing the same as Don and Don walked over, 'I'm looking for Jean, Vic.' Vic looked puzzled, 'I'm looking for Dawn, I was going to check the vegetable gardens, as well. Maybe Dawn is arranging a house for Jean, let's check the empty houses.'

Don and Vic walked around the Square, checking all the empty houses, but there was no sign of the two women. They headed back to Don's house and went inside. Don poured two whiskeys and they sat at the kitchen table.

They were both silent for a while, then Don spoke, 'I think I know where the two of them might have gone. Can we pop back to your place?'

Don and Vic finished their drinks and walked across to Dawn's place.

Don let Vic lead the way in and Vic glanced inside the wash house, 'Don, the coats. Aren't there.' Vic walked into the wash house. The two oversized coats that were painted with slime and used to walk among the dead were gone.

Vic slapped his hand against the wall, 'fuck!'

Vic ran inside the house and came back out with two blankets. He laid them out on the ground and started painting slime over them from a bucket, 'where do you think they may have gone, Don?' Don looked very concerned, 'I think they may have gone to retrieve Jean's daughter's body.'

Vic draped a slime covered sheet over Don, from head to toe and tied it with string around his neck, chest and waist, then did the same for himself.

He had picked up a silenced revolver on the way out and tucked this down his trouser belt.

The two men headed back to Don's house and Don picked up the spike. They ran down the garden, out through the park, then along Beech Grove, onto Schalkschmul Road.

16

A Change in Behaviour

Wayne Stokesly had managed on his own, since the outbreak. He'd taken residence in an upstairs flat above the Ocean Palace Chinese takeaway, not by choice, but because it had an open door and he was running away from around a hundred zombies, at the time.

Wayne was thirty-five years old, single and he had overgrown brown hair and beard. He wore dirty jeans, black trainers, you know, the sort you buy at a supermarket and he wore a grey NYC sweatshirt, which was filthy.

Wayne never changed clothes. Food was Wayne's only priority. He needed nothing else to survive.

Wayne had avoided people, seeing them as a liability to be around and, from a safe distance, he'd witnessed many deaths of people that had dropped their guard, around the dead.

That day, he'd made sure the flat was clear, then watched from the upper window, as the crowd below gradually lost interest and milled away.

Wayne's routine was basic. He'd watch and wait. If there weren't many dead around, he'd make his way down the neighbouring houses, breaking in and taking as much food and drink as he could find. He wouldn't leave the flat for any other reason. He carried a metal bar, he'd found in a neighbouring garage, but very rarely used it. Avoidance was   Wayne's survival strategy and it worked for him.

Wayne had learned, that if in trouble and there was no path back to the flat, he could get into a vehicle and cover himself up. The dead would initially surround the car, but lose interest, when they could not see him, so he always had a blanket in his back pack.

When the dead had laid down, Wayne had gradually gone further afield. He managed to get into the Lion Garage shop, on the front street, where a lock had recently been forced and he had been shuttling back and forth, with as much food and drinks as he could carry, on the day the birds screamed.

On his last run Wayne realised he'd gone out once too often. He'd made a mistake. The dead were on their feet in all directions.

He made along the road and diverted away from a group of dead, that were blocking his path to the Red Lion roundabout. He passed alongside Trinity Church into Clovelly gardens, a cul-de-sac, with dead between him and the houses. There were dead converging from the street into the cul-de-sac entrance.

Wayne quickly tried car doors and managed to get inside a Nissan juke, lying across the back seat and pulling the blanket out of the bag and over the top of him.

He sighed with relief as around fifteen dead bumped against the car and he lay still.

The bumping went on for around five minutes, as normal, but Wayne's relief turned to absolute horror when he heard the click of the car door and felt the breeze from outside.

Two cold hands grabbed his feet and he was dragged out of the car, the blanket, being left behind. His body and head bounced against the frame of the car door as he was pulled out and into the road.

Wayne screamed in agony, as he was bit on his arms, legs, lower body, all at the same time and within a minute, his body was being repeatedly bitten and pulled apart by dozens of hungry dead, all jostling for position to feed.

Dead that had missed out, then made their way towards the houses. As they reached front and side doors, they stood, bumping against them for a while, but, one at a time reached out, took door handles and tried the doors. Others were doing the same with every abandoned car.

* * *

The two women stood silent. Dawn had given Jean strict instructions to follow, if they were going to go on this venture and it was paramount, now that she heeded what she'd been told.

They had left the Square by the park and out onto Beech Grove, when they walked into the horde. Dawn was carrying a baseball bat, but only for use in a last resort.

Around a hundred dead were walking down from the front street and the two women had come out of the Whitley Memorial School entrance right among them. They stood still under the large, slime covered coats, as dead brushed past, some stopping and looking at them and reaching out, as if curious, as to why they stood still, but one after the other, these dead were pushed on, as the horde made their way down Beech Grove.

Jean was terrified and they stood firm against the wall of a house, desperately trying not to be swept away in the flow. She was crying, but knew if she made a sound, they were as good as dead.

Then, it was over. The last of the dead passed and the two women watched them disappear down Beech Grove and past Hirst Villas, out of view.

They walked along to Schalkschmul Road and on, towards the court house, stopping beside the path that led to the alley, where they were headed.

Dawn could see a few dead on the pathway, between them and the alley. She pulled back the hood of the coat and looked at Jean, 'you said she's up there past the sheltered housing place?' 'yes, that's where we had to leave her.'

Dawn put both hands on Jean's shoulders, 'we must stay silent, whatever happens. They can't see us, Jean, so when we get there, we'll wait for the best time and take turns to carry her. Just stand still if more dead come.' Jean nodded, 'thanks, thanks, Dawn, I couldn't leave her here. My child.' Dawn looked Jean in the eyes, 'I know, Jean. I know.'

Dawn's heart sunk, when she saw Katie Allinson's body. She'd been bitten on the left arm and neck and the amount of blood around indicated she'd bled out from the neck wound. There was a puncture wound on the side of her head, where Don had ended her.

Dawn knelt beside the body, carefully lifted the girl to a seated position and Jean knelt down and picked her up. Arms under Katie's back and legs, Jean stood up and they turned and made their way back down the alley. There was only one dead man in their path, slowly walking towards them, so the two women very slowly walked down towards him. Dawn whispered, 'stand to the side when we get to him. Let him pass and when he's passed, I'll take Katie for a while.' Jean nodded and they slowly made their way down the alley.

* * *

Something had come to Phil Burton and he'd grabbed it and eaten. The pain had subsided and the something had gone still and quiet. There was more like this all around, but far out of his reach. They made a lot of noise, though.

Phil was dressed in a white shirt and navy tie, with black trousers, leather black shoes. The citizen watch on his arm was still showing the correct time, but time was nothing to Phil, now. Phil had horrific bites to his arms, chest and neck and the white shirt, was actually mostly the red colour of dried blood.

Phil took another bite, then sat up.

Phil sat for a while, then looked around. The pain in his lower body was coming back. He needed to find something…food.

Phil stood up and looked around. He could see nothing. He put his head to the side. He could hear and smell nothing. The food that was all around, but out of reach earlier was gone, so it was very quiet.

Phil was still holding what he'd eaten earlier, but it was nothing, now, so he dropped it on the ground and he began walking.

There was movement up ahead. Ones like himself, moving around. He stood and focussed on them. None of them were carrying something he could eat. He saw them leave the footpath ahead and onto the road.

Two like himself were making their way in the opposite direction. He could not see if they had something, so he followed and watched from the bottom of the alley, as they stood looking over nothing.

Phil turned to walk away, but turned back. He had no thoughts, but he instinctively made his way towards the two like himself.

As he neared the two like himself. Phil could see one was carrying a large bundle of nothing. He stopped and gazed, turning his head to the side and sniffing, but the one like himself was carrying nothing.

The ones like himself had stopped walking and moved to the side, but Phil stepped towards them. He held out his hand and took hold of the nothing. The one like himself held tight and he raised his hand and grabbed at long strands that were hanging down, but they were nothing.

Phil held out his hand and touched the one like himself. There was a noise. The one like himself was something. The one like himself was food.

* * *

Dawn and Jean carefully approached the zombie and, as he neared, they moved to the side and stood, backs against a wooden fence.

The zombie was dressed, as if on his way to an office, other than the shirt he was wearing was covered in dried blood from massive, deep bites on his chest, neck and arms.

Both women stood silent as he passed, but as he passed, the zombie slowed to a stop and turned towards Jean.

He stepped forward and stood for a while, just staring towards her. He arched his neck to the side and sniffed the air.

Dawn and Jean stood still, fixed to the spot with fear, as the zombie reached out and took Katie's dead hand. He held it for a few moments then let it drop.

The dead man then grabbed Katie's hair and raised it towards his face, gazing and smelling, then let it drop.

Jean stood still and quiet as the dead man stood looking past the girl and into her eyes, under the hood. He reached out and touched Jean's face, with his ice-cold hand and she screamed, quickly stepping back out of his reach.

Katie's body fell to the floor, as the man lunged forward towards Jean.

There was a hollow sounding crack, as Dawn struck the dead man with the baseball bat, but it wasn't hard enough to break the skull.

The man grabbed at Jean and managed to grab her arms, taking Jean to ground and he just ignored the blows raining down on him as he tried to force his face towards the food he'd exposed.

Jean was screaming and desperately trying to keep the man's face from her body, but she was weakening. Dawn was still desperately flailing the bat and, just as Jean's arms collapsed under the weight of the zombie, they heard three spitting sounds.

The dead man collapsed, his body lying flat on top of Jean.

Cold, dark blood and splattered brain ran down her face and chest and she frantically pushed at the body, until it was rolled off her.

Don Mason grabbed and threw the body to the side and took Jean in his arms. Don was wrapped in a slime covered blanket and he quickly removed Jean's coat, checking her for bites.

Jean was in a daze and looked around. Vic Hind was standing alongside Dawn, silenced revolver in his hand.

He put his hand in a shoulder bag he was carrying and pulled out a cotton tea towel. Vic passed it to Dawn, 'clean her up Dawn. Be quick. We need to move.'

Jean was sobbing and Don stepped back, as Dawn knelt beside her, 'She hasn't been bitten, Dawn, thank God.'

Jean was shaking, uncontrollably and rolled to the side and vomited.

Don looked across to Vic and Vic knelt down and took Katie's body in his arms. He looked across, as Dawn was getting Jean to her feet, 'Let's get her home, then Jean. We'll give her a proper funeral.'

Dawn helped Jean back on with the coat and turned to Don and Vic, 'If we encounter dead, we need to put Katie down until they pass. Don this one was curious. We've never seen this, so far. We thought they either see food or nothing.

This one seemed to want to know why we were carrying a dead child. Don, he worked out that Jean wasn't one of them. God help us if that happens with a crowd.'

Don nodded and caught Vic's eye, 'We'll head back the way we came. Let me know when you need a rest and I'll carry Katie.' Vic nodded and they left.

A journey of around half a mile took an hour and a half, as the group continually had to put Katie's body down to let dead pass. Eventually they got to the park and they passed through and into Don's garden.

Don laid Katie's body down in the shed. He'd seen Jamie looking out of the bedroom window and gestured to him not to go into the shed. Jamie nodded and closed the curtains.

The four sat quiet for a while in Don's living room. He poured large brandies and Dawn had to help Jean take a drink.

Jean looked across to Don, 'I'm so sorry, Don, Vic, Dawn, for putting you all in danger. I'm sorry.' She sobbed, bitterly and Dawn put her arms around her and pulled her close.

Don took a large drink and spoke to the two women, 'I understand. I really understand, why you both did what you did. I wouldn't have left Emma out there, but you both know you just had to ask. When we got back, Vic and I, Clarky, Midgy, any of the guys could have gone out and got Katie. My only concern is that we may have lost one or both of you. That would be the tragedy.'

Dawn looked across at Vic and Vic looked back, 'what? don't look at me. I'm nowhere near squeaky clean, but my life is nothing without you, Dawn. Don's right, it isn't safe out there. We need to go quiet at the Square and the farm, for a while. See if this passes and, if the dead go down again, when they run out of food, we've got to clear them away.

My view is that the main thing is we're safe, now. We got back and, Jean, this afternoon we'll lay your daughter to rest. It won't be a cure for how your feeling, I know, but it will be a start.'

Don topped up the drinks and looked around, 'there is a concern I have, if the dead are working things out. I need to go out once more.'

Dawn stayed with Jean, as Vic went to the garden and Don made for Hannah's house.

An hour later, Don, Hannah, Vic, Jean, Dawn and Colleen stood over the open grave, at the bottom of Don's garden. Jamie watched from the bedroom window.

Vic went to the shed. He'd wrapped Katie's body in a white sheet and he carried her across the garden and carefully placed her in the grave.

Don stood with an arm around Jean, who was crying bitterly. He stood silent looking at the hardwood cross Jamie had made for Emma's grave and then alongside at Katie's.

He looked around the group of people and spoke, 'No one should have to bury their young child, but the world has changed. I'm sorry I didn't get to know Katie, but in her time on Earth she was loved and she was taken from those who love her far too soon. May God be with young Katie, as we lay her to rest.'

Vic stepped forward and started filling the grave.

Jean stepped alongside Don and put her arms around him.

Everyone embraced Jean and Don, as they left and Hannah hung back. As Jean went inside Hannah held out a hand and stopped Don, 'Don't go out again, Don, I've got this. I'll go with Vic, instead, don't worry, I know what I need to do. You stay here. Stay with Jean and Jamie. You've had more than enough in the last few days.'

Don was about to argue the case, but the realisation came over him that Hannah was right.

Don was exhausted, physically and mentally drained. His hands were still shaking and his heart pounding, 'alright, Hannah, I'll contact Geordie and Ed, later. I need to get a message to Mark at North Ridge. Ed might send someone. Are you sure you can do what we discussed earlier?' Hannah nodded, 'you know you can count on me, Don.'

Jamie was sat beside Jean in the sitting room when Don came back in the room. He stood up, giving his seat up to Don and made his way to the wash house workshop.

Don called behind him, 'what are you doing Jamie?'

Jamie turned in the doorway, 'We've still got some pieces of hardwood from when I made the cross for Emma's grave. I'm going to make one for Katie's'

Jean got up and walked over. She took Jamie in her arms, held him tight, kissed him and, through her tears said, 'thank you, thank you son. I'd like that.'

Vic and Dawn arrived home and sank into the settee. Vic had thrown the coats and blankets into the front garden to put away later. He was too tired to do anything more.

They were quiet for a while and Vic broke the silence, 'Dawn, what the fuck were you thinking? I could have lost you.' Dawn sat head down, 'I went to see her, Vic, when you all left. She was broken. Vic, she would have gone on her own.

She was half way down Don's garden when I got there. The thing is, Vic, I don't think she had planned to come back.'

Vic pulled Dawn close, thank God you got back. After the last few days…' He shed a tear and gasped for breath, 'after the last few days, I don't think I'd manage without you.'

The two kissed and sat cuddled together and Dawn looked him in the eyes, 'let's hope the troubles are over, then and we don't have to go out any more for a good while.'

There was a knock at the front door.

17

Drop Off and Collection

Dawn answered the door and called back to Vic, 'it's Hannah.' She stepped to the side, 'please come in, love and have a seat, we're in the living room. Can I get you some tea?'

Hannah smiled awkwardly and shook her head.

Hannah didn't sit down. She knew what she was going to ask of Vic wouldn't go down too well with Dawn.

She spoke to Vic, 'I'm going outside again. I've spoken with Don and he told me the dead are showing curiosity, behaving differently. If that's the case, we need to let the men in Breakers know.

Their security gate is only locked by a chain and tent peg and the kids living there, go out on a regular basis. I also need to get to the two women at Millfield. They think they're safe and secure, there, but if the dead find a way in, they could walk right into them.

Don is going to contact Ed at Nedderton, by walkie and ask him to get a message to a survivor we found at North Ridge. He said he'll contact Geordie at the farm, later, as well.

I've come to ask you to come with me. I'm worried about Don, Vic, he's exhausted. I don't think he should go out again.'

Hannah was right about Dawn and Dawn immediately rounded on her, 'Don's exhausted? And Vic isn't? Vic hasn't been to bed since the night before last. We're all tired, Hannah. What about the others? Can't one of the others go out with you? Maybe Midgy, Dowser or one of the younger men?'

Hannah nodded, 'I've asked Paul Dawson to come. There're a few things to drop off at Breakers, so I need a hand with the trailer.'

Dawn shook her head, 'you're going to take a trailer up the front street, through a horde of dead?' Hannah nodded, 'I've done it before and there are provisions at the house at Millfield, that will replenish the stores. I'll cover the trailer with slimed blankets, over polythene sheeting. We can step aside if the dead get curious. It's worth the risk.'

Hannah turned and left the room. She glanced back at Dawn, 'your right, Dawn, I've got no right to ask Vic to come with me after what he's been through. It was selfish of me. I came here because I knew my best chance of getting back here in one piece would be if Vic was with me. I will ask the others.

When I left Don's house Dowser and Paul were on their way to see him. I'll go back and ask Dowser or knock on Midgy.'

Dawn put her hand on her brow and looked at Vic, who was standing up. She knew Vic had decided to go with Hannah and Dawn put her arms around him, 'you're going, aren't you?'

Vic kissed Dawn on the lips, 'the dead are behaving differently. I have to see what we're up against. Hannah's right, I can get them there and back and I can get them out, if it goes bad.'

Hannah left the house and picked up one of the slime covered overcoats, that had been left in the front garden. Paul was walking along the middle of the road, carrying the machete.

Vic put the blanket back on and tucked the silenced revolver into his belt. He passed the other overcoat to Paul and then took the bucket at the end of the garden and painted more slime on the coats. Hannah reciprocated, covering the blanket that was tied to Vic.

Colleen was stood at the door, as the three pushed the trailer off the drive and into the Square. Hannah stepped towards Colleen and Colleen shook her head, 'no fucking way, blow me one.' Hannah puckered her lips and blew a kiss to Colleen and baby Amelia.

There was a call from inside the house. It was Bob Rice. He stepped up behind Colleen, 'be careful out there, Hannah.'

Hannah held up a hand and the group made their way along to the gates, opened up and they left the square, locking the gate behind them.

Vic and Paul began pushing. The trailer was light, but there was something on board. He lifted the blanket and saw three petrol driven generators, two large petrol cans and a sealed cardboard box.

There was an envelope taped to the carrying handle of one of the generators and there was a padlock on the trailer floor.

Right away Vic noticed something different and stopped, they had only got as far as adjacent to the Black Bull pub. The others looked at him and he whispered, 'look around, the cars. Look at all the open doors.'

Cars all along the street had one or more open doors.

They made their way further along and Vic stopped again. A zombie was coming out of a house on Vicarage Terrace and it made its way to the next and began bumping against the door.

Vic whispered again, 'none of those doors have been open, when we've passed. It's found an unlocked door, Jesus.'

The three encountered a few dead, but not many, as they slowly made their way past the Northumberland Arms, but there was a large horde making their way past the Market Cross towards the Red Lion and small groups of dead were joining them and following.

Vic Paul and Hannah, used this as an opportunity and they kept well back, slowly following the horde, until they got to the gate at Breakers.

Paul carefully opened the gate and Hannah and Vic took down a group of dead, that hadn't kept up with the horde, which was, by now walking over the Red Lion roundabout.

Vic had taken Paul's machete and chopped through three heads and Hannah spiked three more, with her spiked rounders bat.

Paul offloaded the generators, petrol and the taped-up cardboard box and quickly closed the gate and chain, this time inserting and locking the padlock. He threw the keys to the padlock against the door, well out of reach of the gate and then the three of them turned the empty trailer around and made their way down the street, for Church lane.

Church lane was a challenge. There were numerous dead coming out of gardens and driveways. Hannah and Paul took them down, as Vic pushed the trailer.

About half way down Church lane Vic let the trailer go. It freewheeled about twenty feet, towards a massive group of dead and Vic, Hannah and Paul slowly walked into entrance to Towers Close, a small estate that leads to a dead end, behind St Cuthbert's Church. They watched from behind an abandoned car.

The group of around thirty dead walked around the trailer, repeatedly touching the sides and handle, then some of them commenced lifting the blankets and looking under. Vic looked at Hannah and Paul, 'They're searching.'

In around ten minutes the dead slowly lost interest, left and soon caught up the massive crowd, making their way along Church lane, towards Millfield South.

When they were out of sight, Hannah, Don and Paul continued with the trailer, heading for the west entrance to Millfield.

Hannah stopped at the two large adjoined stone houses, The Tower and the Beeches. She looked through a closed metal gate.

The houses were set within their own grounds, but the doors were wide open and a lot dead were wandering around the drive and garden. There were pieces of black bird parts scattered around, lots of this and Hannah imagined there would be many more dead inside the houses.
It certainly wasn't a safe place to further investigate.

Vic could see a small group of dead, coming down Church lane, from the road leading to the farm, but the vastly larger crowd had made their way down Millfiled South, away from them.

Hannah stood by the barrier of cars blocking the entrance to Millfield and Vic held up a hand, 'there's a few dead making their way along towards us. Quite a way down so we have a good amount of time. Paul and I will take them down, if they get here, before we've loaded up. Hannah, you go seek the women.'
Hannah passed the spiked rounders bat to Vic and ran to the house that Amanda and Cynthia had occupied.

Cynthia came to the door and called for Amanda, who had been taking a nap. The two stood in the doorway, and Hannah spoke, 'Don Mason has sent me. He wants the two of you to come with us. I have a trailer at the barrier for the supplies.

It's important you come. We've seen a change in the behaviour of the dead. We don't think you're safe.'

Cynthia glanced at Amanda, who quickly replied, 'yes, yes we'll come. Thank you. Come in, there are bin liners in the cupboard. We can pack bags with all the food and drinks, it won't take long. Alec Donaldson had a lot of DVD's and computer games. He also had weapons. I'll clear upstairs, if you two empty the kitchen and, Cyn, don't forget the wine rack in the wash house.'

The three women quickly shuttled bags of goods to the trailer, then Cynthia closed the front door for the last time.

As they got to the barrier, Vic held up a hand, 'wait there, Hannah, they're here.' Four dead men rounded the corner and made straight for Vic and Paul. In seconds they had all been taken down and the two men came back and held out hands to help the women over the barrier.

As Amanda jumped down into the road, she stood frozen to the spot, 'oh God.'

The group turned and looked across towards Church lane. A young dead girl was walking towards them. She had long blonde hair and was wearing leggings and a yellow puffer jacket, zipped up to the top.

Cynthia started to cry, 'it's the girl from the video. Alec Donaldson raped and murdered her. He filmed her rising from the dead from the window.

Hannah stepped forward with the bat, but quickly stepped back. There was another dead woman, making her way around the corner, behind the young girl.

Sharon Thompson was a few feet behind the girl. Her arms, legs, chest and neck were covered in deep wounds. Cynthia gasped in horror and Amanda started crying.

The two dead approached and Vic took out the silenced revolver. He fired once and the young girl in the yellow jacket, fell dead. He raised the gun again and Paul held up a hand, 'let me.' Paul walked over to Sharon Thompson and with one swipe of the machete, Sharon was decapitated.

Paul looked across at Cynthia and Amanda, 'I…I'm…' Amanda looked up, ''It's alright, Paul. She deserved no less.'

Vic walked onto Church lane. There were no dead in sight, but as he returned, he could see the large horde they had seen earlier, passing the barrier at the east side of Millfield.

The others looked across at the crowd, beyond the far barrier. Vic addressed the group, 'the way I see it is that this lot are headed for the Front street. If we follow their path, a safe distance behind, we should be ok. Our best route is down Millfield South.' They all agreed and set off into Church lane.

As the group started pushing the trailer, Vic called out, 'stop! What the fuck?'

A large dog was running across the Twenty Acre field towards them. It was barking and snarling. Cynthia stepped back, 'it's a Rottweiler, how the Hell has it survived?'

Vic stepped in front of the trailer and stood with his arm across his chest, resting the barrel of the revolver on it. The dog was still barking and snarling, as it left the field and ran over the road, towards him. He fired three times and the dog gave out a high-pitched yelp, then fell dead, blood running out of head neck and side wounds.

Paul looked through the barrier, across Millfield, 'the dead, they've heard the fucking dog. They're at the barrier.'

The group watched as the cars in the barrier began to give way to the crowd pushing against it and, as the barrier gave way, hundreds of dead flooded into Millfield, trampling over the ones who had been crushed in the push.

Vic called out, 'we have to go.' The three women began pushing the barrow, as quickly as they could and Vic and Paul jogged alongside, Paul holding the Machete and Vic the pistol and club.

They ran along Millfield South and, as they got to the end, Vic signalled to stop and ran along to the barrier the dead had pushed in.

The dead were half way across Millfield. Vic waved and the group pushed hard, quickly passing Millfield Court and down onto the Front street.

They made their way up the main road, running past wandering dead, who immediately turned and followed. Vic called out, 'Cynthia, Amanda, you must run ahead, they can see you both, keep close to me.'

Vic ran up, unlocked the gate and held it open, for Cynthia and Amanda. The others followed with the trailer. Vic was unable to close the gate and ten dead stumbled through. He fired the revolver four times, then it was empty.

Four zombies fell with headshots, as Hannah and Paul bludgeoned the others, with the club and machete. Soon the ten zombies lay still in the entrance.

Hannah went outside the gate and called to the others, 'quick, we need to drag the bodies over the road. We can't leave them inside.'

More dead were making their way down the street, but the Hannah and the others managed to drag the ten bodies out of the entrance and over to the overgrown verges across the road, just in time to get the gate closed.

Hannah chained and padlocked the gate and they all stopped for breath, looking up as four more dead arrived.

Vic stepped closer, as the dead bumped against the gate for a few minutes. One of the dead, a middle-aged man then reached out to the chain and pulled against it, then let it drop. He reached out again and took the padlock in his hand and pulled it against the chain. Two more dead had taken hold of the bars of the gate and were rattling it back and forth.

Vic and the others turned and wheeled the trailer into the Square. They dropped the slime coats in Vic's garden, then took the trailer down to the store house and walked over to Don's house. He'd seen them through the window and was at the front door.

Within a few minutes, Hannah and Paul had knocked on all the doors at the square and all the residents gathered round outside Don's house.

Dawn had both arms around Vic and Colleen and Hannah stood side by side. Paul had joined Marie.

Don stood alongside Amanda and Cynthia and addressed the residents. 'You all know we've had trouble with a relation of the Donaldsons. The trouble was caused by Sharon Thompson.'
Vic spoke up, 'she's dead now, Don. We all saw her. Paul put her to rest.'

Don nodded and continued, 'I asked Cynthia, Amanda and Sharon to leave the square, when we took Donaldson down, but things have changed.

This morning, when we confronted our children's kidnapper, Amanda Blewitt saved Paul Dawson's life. She risked her own life to prevent Sharon Thompson from shooting him.

She also gave evidence to Ken Martin. That showed the Donaldsons in their true light. I won't make a decision without consulting the residents, here, but things are changing outside.

The dead are much more dangerous than before. I'm asking for your consent to give a home to Cynthia and Amanda.'

Dowser spoke up, 'the threat to us was the Thompson girl. She wanted revenge and it eventually got her killed. I think these two just want a safe home. I say let them stay.'

Ted Knight stepped forward. He was unrecognisable from when he'd been rescued. He was clean, his hair was cut and tidy and he was wearing Levi 501 jeans and a navy Hilfiger hoody.

The girls had been to work on him. He spoke up, 'I've only just arrived here, but our Julie has told me all about the troubles you've all had. I have to say, I'd rather die than go back out there and I expect these girls know the value of a safe place to live, by now. It sounds like they had no say in matters that went on before, so, in my eyes, they have as much right as me to be here. Let them stay.'

Clarky stepped forward, 'Dowser and Ted are right, Don. The feud is over. We all have the same enemy, now. I'll make this easy, anyone against giving these two a safe home?'

No one opposed. Clarky stepped back, 'there, we have it. Welcome to Hollymount Square.'

Amanda looked around, then spoke, 'Whatever has gone on before, I want you all to know it's over. My husband was a monster and I never knew. I thought he just followed Ray Donaldson, but I stumbled on what he'd been doing and, I could never forgive...' She started to cry and Cynthia continued, 'our husbands and Sharon's were involved in Alec Donaldson's crimes against young girls. They both deserved to die.'

Cynthia looked at Clarky, 'whatever happened to Sammy and Abe, that day, Ian, I know now they deserved it. I hope you know we weren't ever aware of their crimes, until Amanda found that camera.'

Clarky walked over and took Amanda Blewitt in his arms, 'it's over, now. The two of you are home. Thank you for what you did this morning.'

There was one more voice, as the residents were dispersing. 'Before everyone leaves, we've overlooked something, Don.' Jean had come to the front door, 'you said the dead are working things out. Remember, we just made it into the park.

There were dead behind us. What if...'

Don turned and looked back, 'oh God, the exits in the fence. I need to get there right away.'

Hannah turned to the residents, 'everyone needs to get home, lock down and keep quiet. We have to go into the park. There may be dead, I'm coming with you. Don.' A number of voices all at once, called out that they would come and within a few minutes, the residents had returned home and eight residents were watching on, as Don slid back the fence panel at the bottom of his garden.

18

Welfare Park

Don addressed the group just inside the park, 'Hannah and Chris, you go round the perimeter along the Haig Road side, Vic and I will make our way to the entrance hatch beside the school. The rest of you, go straight to the bowling green. If there're dead in your way, take them down. We have to assume they have worked the sliding panel out.

When I secure the panel in the fence, we all meet at the bowling green and make some noise.

We have to draw them out and make sure that when were done, there are no dead left walking around in here.'

Vic had loaded both silenced revolvers and passed one to Clarky.

Hannah and Chris made their way along the perimeter fence, as Vic and Don went the other way. They could see no dead, but the grass was long, so they were cautious and took their time.

Clarky led Dowser, Paul, Midgy and Ronnie, slowly through the long grass, towards the bowling green.

As Don and Vic neared the exit, they could see a zombie, clumsily trying to crawl through the gap in the fence, eventually falling through, flat on its face. The panel was open. Vic fired a shot which spat from the revolver, into the dead man's head. He dragged the body to one side, as Don closed up the panel and reached into a shoulder bag.

Don pulled out a cordless screwdriver, then quickly secured the panel with two - inch screws. Don looked up, 'they're in here.'

The two made their way back around the park path towards the bowling green, keeping a wide berth from trees and shrubs.

Within a few minutes all nine of them were stood on the bowling green.

The grass was overgrown, but still quite short, having gone to seed, just above ankle deep.

Clarky held the revolver in both hands, 'I've seen some dead, over there. They seem to be making their way around the fence, There's a few around the pavilion.' Hannah also spoke, 'we saw a few at the Bedlington Terriers club house, trying doors.'

The group stood in the middle of the bowling green and Paul Dawson took Hannah's club and banged the machete against it. Paul handed Hannah the club back and the group, together, looked in all directions.

Vic and Clarky were ready with revolvers, Don had the spike, Paul the Machete and the rest were carrying baseball bats. Vic cautioned everyone, 'Only go for one if we can't shoot them all. Minimal risk, everyone.'

There was silence for a few moments, then rustling of shrubs and long grass. Zombies were making their way towards the bowling green from every direction. There were around thirty.

Hannah looked at Don, 'holy shit!' Vic called out, 'be ready! there aren't enough rounds in the revolvers, Clarky, take down as many as you can!' As the dead converged on the group there was repeated spitting of silenced gunshots. Some shots took zombies down, but there were a few deflections and misses, then the rounds ran out.

There were still around fifteen dead and they continued to close in.

It was carnage, as the baseball bats, clubs and machete were repeatedly swung at the dead and, within a few minutes there were only two zombies left, that had been struck, but survived the blows.
Vic patted Don on the back, 'it's done.' Both dead were struggling to get back up and Hannah stepped towards a middle-aged woman. Paul stood over a young man, wielding the machete.

Hannah swung the club and the spike penetrated the woman's head through the temple and she fell for the last time.

Paul hesitated though. The man, around mid - twenties had nearly got back to his feet and looked up at Paul. Dowser called out, 'Paul! Hit him, Paul!' but Paul stood motionless and dropped the Machete.

Just as the young dead man gained his balance and grabbed for Paul, Don ran across and spiked him through the side of the head. Paul fell to his knees and Dowser quickly knelt alongside him, 'Paul, what happened, you could have…' 'It was Quinten dad.' Paul started to cry and Dowser looked down at the man's body, 'Quinten's Paul's best mate, I'm sorry, son, so sorry, I didn't...'

Paul sobbed, hands over his face and Dowser sat with him. There was nothing Dowser could say to console his son.

In a few minutes, Paul stood up, 'I, I can't leave him here, dad.' Dowser put an arm around him, 'come on, we can bury him at the bottom of our garden. There's plenty space.' The two picked up Quinten's body, by arms and legs and the group made their way back to Don's house.

Don screwed the panel in his fence closed and they stood together in the garden. Dowser addressed the others, 'we'll lay Quinten to rest. I think we all need a break, here.'

Don held up a hand, 'before everyone leaves, we need to get the word around again to lock down, no one out.'

Vic spoke, 'I don't think anyone will be wanting to do anything more today, Don, except the kids, maybe. I think Dawn wants them to offload the trailer. There may be some well - earned treats on board. There's still a bit of time before it gets too dark.'

Earlier, Dawn had gone into the store house and come back out with a bunch of keys, but when the group had left, she'd taken Cynthia and Amanda to her place and made tea. On Vic's return she'd gone back out and rounded up all the kids in the Square.

She stood on the garden wall of the store house and shouted out, 'right, all you kids step forward! We need this trailer off loaded and you kids are going to do it. Your reward will be all the sweets you can eat.'

Dawn pulled the blankets and some plastic covers off the trailer, uncovering a full load of packed bin bags, containing sweets, crisps and snacks of all sorts, pop and a multitude of canned foods.

Dawn looked at Vic, who had a massive smile on his face, 'a handful of you pushed all this through a horde of zombies?' Vic laughed, 'look at their faces, Dawn. I'd say reasonable risk, wouldn't you?'

Dawn gave Vic a stern look, 'nothing like the risk of what might happen to you when I get you home, Vic Hind.' She called out, 'The DVD's go to my place for movie night and no drinking alcohol, kids!'

As all the kids converged on the trailer, Dawn walked over to Cynthia and Amanda, 'come on, then. Let's find you both a house.' Amanda reached into the trailer and pulled out two back packs, 'these are ours.' One of them clanked as two of the numerous bottles of Cava came together. The three women all looked at each other and laughed. Dawn rattled the keys, 'looks like we need a house with three glasses.'

Hannah was the last person away from Don's. She was shaking and Don stood beside her, 'you ok?' Hannah reached out, cuddled into Don and started crying, 'I was so scared, Don.

The number of dead that came after us at Millfield. It was…'

Don held her close, 'thank God you're safe, Hannah, all of you. I don't think I'm the only one who needs a break here, flower. It's been the hardest day since…We lock down now Hannah. No one leaves the square. We have a mountain of food, drinks and all the gardens are planted with veg, that will last us months.'

Hannah set off for home and Don went back inside and sat in his armchair. Jean had gone to the window and was watching the kids offloading the trailer, 'they're eating as much as they're carrying in, there Don.' Don smiled, 'they can only eat so much, though, Jean, Dawn knows exactly what she's doing.'

Paul Dawson cried, as he and his dad lowered Quinten into the hole they'd dug at the bottom of the garden. He looked up at his mother, 'I never put his name down on the list. mum. I never thought about anyone but us, I…' Angie Dawson took Paul in her arms, and he sobbed against her shoulder, 'you had to ensure you got Marie to safety and us, Paul. You were looking out for us, as well. Look at Quinten, look Paul, the blood and dirt is dried on and look at his skin and wounds. Paul, I'd say Quinten has been dead a long time. You couldn't have saved him, son.'

Marie took Paul's hand, 'let's say our goodbyes and cover him up. He's at rest now. You need to clean up, you and your dad, then we'll have a strong drink. We'll raise a glass to Quinten.'

A few doors along the road, Don poured two large whiskies, as Jean prepared jam and bread. When she brought it through, Don was asleep. Jean lay down on the settee. They could have the jam and bread later.

It was ten o'clock when Don woke up. Jamie had returned home and gone to his room, but there was a box of Cadbury's Roses on the coffee table, alongside the two large whiskeys and jam and bread. Jean was still asleep.

Don went into the kitchen and took a walkie. He needed to talk to Geordie and Ed to make sure they were fully aware of the new dangers, outside.

Geordie was first to reply, 'yes, Don, we've seen a change. The dead are back and forward along the road. We're keeping quiet, when it's a large group and the kids are taking them down with the catapults and ball bearings, from the top of the stacks if just a few.
We have noticed, they're walking around as much of the perimeter as they can access, looking for a way in. It's like they suspect there's something behind the walls.'

Ed came on the walkie, 'Eustace has been over to the North Ridge boy. He offered a home over here, but Eustace says he's a troubled soul. Wants to live this out alone. He knows the dead are changing.

Eustace stayed a while and helped him reinforce the barriers. Don, we've seen some dead down on the farm land. First time I've seen them venture away from the streets, without a reason.'

Geordie spoke next, 'yes, Don, odd ones are appearing out of the woods and plantation, where there's gaps in the fencing. They had no interest in the woods before. We've got kids doing hour long shifts, watching with binoculars all daylight hours.

Don spoke once more, 'well take care everyone. Lock down and stay quiet. Ed, if need be, you know to come down here?' 'Same goes for you Don, Geordie, if it gets bad, make your way here. Ed out.'

Ed and Geordie were finished the call and Don held on to the walkie. After five minutes, or so he engaged the speaker, 'are you there Harvey?'

19

Meanwhile at Breakers

Harvey had woken up around eight o'clock and carried three seats from the bar, to the window. He'd left the fourth seat. Bobby Taylor was still sat at it, sprawled over the bar, beside a half bottle of Lamb's Navy Rum.

Harvey whispered under his breath, 'I towld him to lay off the rum,' then Bobby woke with a start, 'what, what, now?'

Harvey patted Bobby on the back and said, 'just in time, Bobby, lad. Squort's preparing a full English for wis.'

Bobby dragged his bar stool over to the window and took a seat, looking out over Bedlington Front Street.

Willy and Evan made their way across, and also took their seats and Squirt and Happy walked over from behind the bar, carrying four paper plates of food between them.

All the men had the same clothes they had worn for the last week, except Willy. One of the kids had got him a Newcastle away top, you know the nice dark blue one, with the orange shoulder stripes, from a few years ago and he sat, chuffed, regardless that the name on the back, read, 'Marshall' and the number was 'five.'

Willy smiled at the others and held the front of the shirt, as if he needed to pull it away from his body to show them, 'what do you think, lads? Young Cockney got this for me, when they were out, the other day. Says he's got another. Good lad, young Cockney.'

Cockney was lying at the far end of the room, alongside the other kids. He whispered to Robbie, 'they call me Cockney, but I'm from Nottingham. I don't get it.'

Willie had overheard and called over, 'anyone South of Middlesbrough's a Cockney, young un. Anyone south of the smog.' The kids all went into raptures of laughter.

Happy and Squirt laid the plates in front of each man, then returned to the far end of the room, joining all the kids, who were laid out in sleeping bags all over the floor, but awake and chatting.

Harvey was the last to take his seat and put four bottles of Corona on the window sill, one beside each plate. He passed round plastic forks and smiled, 'you can't beat a full English, lads,' the others agreed, 'aye,' 'aye,' 'aye.'

Each plate had a breakfast, consisting of cold tinned tomatoes, cold beans, two cold hot dog sausages, a pickled egg and a pile of Bacon Bites. There were two breadsticks on the side of each plate and Harvey dipped one in the tomato juice and took a bite, as he looked outside.

It was an uneventful day. The men had told the kids to stay put, so there were games of cards going on. The pool tables were busy and a battery powered ghetto blaster was playing dance music over in the girls end, at a reasonable volume.

The men watched out the window, all day, drinking bottled beers and looking for dead people they may recognise.

Outside there were quiet spells, with not many dead in sight, then periods where they were all over the street.

'That fucker's just opened a car door, Harve.' Willy had stood up and pulled the blind further open. At the far side of the road a dead man had opened the door of an abandoned ford fiesta and was bent over, looking inside.

Harvey stood up and stood alongside Willy, watching on.

Evan also opened the blind further in front of him, 'another one is trying the doors across the road, at Job Centre Plus.'

Harvey called Squirt and Happy over, 'you need to see this, kids.' All the kids went to the windows and watched, as dead were searching for food. The dead looked under cars, tried doors and rummaged through anything lying around.

Harvey spoke up, 'this tells wis that yee lot need to be very careful oot there. Nee more jaunts and nee playing aboot, oot there. Thars plenty food, so I want yis ti keep indoors, until we know it's safe.'

He glanced at Squirt, 'son, I mean it. It's too risky oot there. Make sure word gans roond that war waiting for the deed to run oot of bait again, before gannin oot.'

Squirt nodded and the kids all returned to their pastimes.

The men had drunk beer all morning and Willy was carrying four bottles of Budweiser over, when Evan called out, 'is that our Malcolm?'

Bobby put his head closer to the window, 'you mean the big fellow, with the ginger hair and the army jacket on?' 'aye.'

Harvey commented, 'aye, Evan, it's Malky from the Hartlands, I recognise him.'

Willy put the bottles down, 'Malky, from the Hartlands, I haven't seen him since we played footer together, which one?' Evan pointed, 'the one in the combat jacket, it's our Malky.'

Harvey picked up a pair of binoculars and focussed them on Malcolm's feet, 'he's got summit taped ti the bottom of his foot. Looks like a plastic toy. One of them ones yi hoy for the dog.'

He passed the binoculars to Evan and Evan had a look, 'aye, it looks like one of them that squeaks. How the Hell did that get there. Probably why the others are following him.?' One after the other the men replied, 'Aye,' aye,' 'aye.'

Willy looked at Evan, 'fucking hell, Evan, Malky's put some beef on, hasn't he?' 'aye.'

They all sat quiet for a few moments, as Malcolm passed by, at the front of a crowd of about eighty dead, walking towards the Red Lion roundabout. He was around forty-five years old, over six-foot, tall, thick curled ginger hair and around twenty stone, plus. Malcolm's front was covered in blood. It looked fresh.

There were wounds on Malcom's face and side of head, that looked like they may have been failed attempts to take him down, at some time. Harvey was first to comment, 'Malky might be overweight, but the same lad, though, Evan, same lad had managed to save up a four chin, for his retirement,' then Bobby, 'aye the same lad, though, Evan, same lad had a rough upbringing, always had a lot on his plate,' then Willie, 'aye the same lad would leave no one with clearing up to do after a buffet,' then Evan,

'aye, the same lad had high standards, he never just settled on seconds,'
'aye,' 'aye,' 'aye.'

After a couple more beers, the men were sat silent. The pool playing had stopped and the kids had all gone back over to the store area and were sharing out food. Most were sitting on top of sleeping bags, or at tables, eating.

Harvey stood up and pulled open the blind, 'wee's she wee?' Evan replied, 'wee's wee wee?'

The kids broke out into giggles all around, all except Cockney. Even Happy was laughing.

Squirt looked at Cockney, and shook his head.

Cockney was completely straight faced, 'I don't get it. I don't even know what they're saying.' The kids all laughed again.

Squirt glanced at the men, who were all huddled against the window, then back at Cockney, 'in Northumbrian pitmatic slang the word 'wee' has a few meanings. It could mean 'we,' as in 'us,' 'wee,' as in what you might say on a fairground ride and 'wee,' as in 'little.' It could also mean 'who?' and it could mean 'with,' or even 'piss.' In this case Harve asked, 'who is she with?' And Evan asked in reply, 'who is who with?' Am I clear?'

There were giggles all around again and Cockney looked puzzled.

Robbie got to his feet and walked over to the pool table, 'right everyone, wee am I playing pool wee?' All together the kids called out, 'wee's wee playing pool wee?'

There were raptures of laughter all around and Harvey looked over his shoulder, then back out of the window, 'I'm sure there's summit wrang with some of them kids,' 'aye,' 'aye,' 'aye.'

Harvey sat back, 'there, can yis see? three of them, pushing a big barra.' Evan took a closer look, 'it's that lassie, the one that was here the other day. They're keeping back from that crowd, the one Malky was in. Looks like they're coming here. They're opening the gate.

Now they're off loading the barrow. Looks like they've left us stuff.'

There was chatter among the kids and some started running towards the doors. Harvey screamed out, 'you fucking stop right there!'

The kids stopped and the bar went silent.

Harvey walked over and lowered his voice, this time speaking in the Queen's English, 'listen, they attracted dead over, before leaving. If you lot go running out there, you could be pulled through the bars, now settle down and we do this properly.'

It was the first time the kids had heard Harvey talking out of his pitmatic accent. It was also the first time he'd raised his voice at them.

The kids lined up all the way down the stairs and Squirt carefully opened the outer doors. Harvey was right. Five zombies were reaching through the bars, trying to reach the equipment, that had been left.

One thing at a time, Squirt carefully passed the goods back, but one of the dead men had managed to reach through and pull a generator back to the gate.

Squirt turned and called back, 'Harv, I can't get one of them, it's beside the gate. I'm not going…'

Squirt felt someone brush past him. It was Rebecca. She had made her way, between the line of kids, down the stairs, unnoticed.

Before Squirt could grab her, Rebecca stepped forward, just outside the reach of the dead. She stood still and looked at the five men and, within seconds, they simultaneously pulled their arms back through the gate and fencing, then stood up.

Squirt was gobsmacked, as Rebecca continued to look at the dead and, again, simultaneously, they put their heads to the side, as if listening. Then they turned and set off walking down the front street.

Squirt grabbed Rebecca and carried her back inside the door. Harvey was there and he took Rebecca's hand and led her up the stairs.

Squirt grabbed the generator and carried it in. He passed it on, then picked up the padlock keys, that were in the doorway and quickly closed and locked the door.

Everyone stood around the equipment that Hannah and the others had left. Evan pulled the envelope off one of the generators, opened it up and read it out.

'Dear Harvey,

Just a note of thanks for taking us in when we were in a tight spot. I noticed you had no electricity, so I have sent three low noise generators and a supply of petrol. Hopefully this will provide you with light, hot water and the means to get the bandits and computer games going for the kids. You have probably noticed, yourselves that the dead are trying doors and behaving differently, so we have attached a padlock to your gate. The keys should be with the equipment.

I sent two revolvers in the cardboard box and ammunition. If there is anyone else out there like the Donaldson boy, the guns will give you a better chance of keeping them out.

Unfortunately, Connor didn't make it back to Hollymount square, he was bitten, while helping us escape from a tight situation and gave his life to enable us to get home.

Harvey, I have left a two-way radio in the engine hatch of one of the generators. I will be in touch, soon, but please take care and warn the kids, it is very dangerous out there, so much so, we are locking down for a while. I suggest you do the same.

Don.

Squirt passed the padlock keys to Harvey.

Harvey walked over and hung the keys on a hook behind the bar. He looked over to the kids, who were just waiting for the word to get the electric games going and said, 'what yis waiting for, then. Gan and get things running.'

The kids ran in all directions and Harvey called out, 'Rebecca!'

Rebecca walked over and Harvey picked her up by the waist and sat her on the pool table.

The other men watched on from beside the window.

Rebecca smiled at Harvey, 'you smell of beer. There's toothpaste and soap and stuff in the lady's toilet. You could wash. Your clothes smell, as well.'

Harvey took Rebecca's hand. His pitmatic accent was gone again. 'I promise, after our chat, I'll wash up and I'll find some fresh clothes on the pile, ok?' 'ok.'

Harvey thought for a moment then pulled his stool over. He sat down and took Rebecca's hand again, 'what happened down there, Rebecca, love? You know you aren't supposed to go outside and you walked right in front of those dead men.'

Rebecca put her head down then looked back up, 'Squirt couldn't get to the equipment. I had to help him, so I went downstairs.' 'Rebecca, it's dangerous outside. We should have left it there. We can't risk you or Squirt or anyone getting hurt.'

Rebecca looked in Harvey's eyes, 'all I had to do was get them to leave,' 'how, Rebecca? How did you get them to leave?' 'I just told them to go.'

Harvey ran his fingers through his hair, 'I was there Rebecca, you said nothing,' 'I know, but I thought it and they heard.'

Harvey now held Rebecca's hand in both his, 'Rebecca, do you hear their thoughts?' Rebecca laughed, 'no, Harvey, they don't have thoughts. They know they have to eat, that's all. All they see is food and others like themselves. Everything else is nothing to them.

I didn't think in words, I just imagined myself walking away and they did the same. They don't see me as food, Harvey, not anymore.'

Harvey helped Rebecca down from the pool table, 'just one more thing, Rebecca, the dead, they're trying doors, searching. Do you know how this is happening?'

Rebecca shrugged her shoulders, 'no, but I know it isn't nice for them when they go hungry. Maybe they're so desperate to eat, they're looking harder?'

The men sat quiet for about half an hour, then Harvey opened the box and laid the guns on the windowsill. Willy took one in his hand, 'I've shot one of these, in the cadets. I'll show you all how they work.'

Harvey held up a hand, 'coont me ooot, ahm gannin for a wesh.' He made his way over to a large pile of clothes at the far corner of the room and rummaged about, until he found something that would fit.

Twenty minutes later, Harvey winked as he passed Rebecca. His hair was wet and a lot whiter than before and he was wearing a clean blue Adidas hoodie and grey joggers. He'd found a pair of size eight adidas trainers and Rebecca laughed as he pointed at them on the way past.

Harvey sat back down, beside the others and Bobby glanced at him. 'Date on Harve?'

Harvey took a drink out of his bottle and glanced back, 'aye, that lassie from Hollymoont, ah think she fancies is.'

Bobby gave Harvey an assured look, 'aye, she'll be back, Harve. Never lose it, son.' Evan and Willie looked across at Harvey, 'aye,' 'aye.'

After an hour or so, the kids had got things going. Squirt walked over to the window seats, carrying a tray. There were four pints of lager on the tray and the men took one each. Squirt smiled, as the men took a drink and pulled grimaces, 'it'll take a while for the coolers, Harve, but it should get better,' 'I fucking hope so, Squort, there's ownly Cockney in here, that cud stomach warm beer.' Squirt smiled, 'there's a good few barrels in the cellar room. I'll sort it.'

A little later, Cockney walked over to Willie, carrying a carrier bag and all the kids gathered round, in anticipation. He handed Willie the bag and stepped back, 'there you go, Willy, as promised, the other top I got you.'

Willy was near to tears, 'hey, thanks son, you're a canny kid, for a Cockney.' He put his hand in the bag and, as he pulled the contents out there were howls of laughter all round. Willy pulled out a red and white Sunderland top.
Willy was gobsmacked. Harvey, Evan and Bobby shook their heads and laughed.

It took a while, but Willy eventually caved in and had a good laugh, as well. He held his pint up to Cockney, 'nice one, sunner, nice one,' then opened the upper window and threw the top out.

A dead man walked over and picked up the Sunderland top, holding it up in front of his face and Squirt shouted out, 'look, Willy's found a dead Mackem.' Cockney called out, 'wee has?' and the kids howled with laughter.

20

The Intruder

It was eleven thirty pm and the Square had locked down and gone quiet. Unfortunately, baby Amelia wasn't aware of this rule and had been wide awake for two hours, crying every time Colleen and Hannah had put her down to sleep.

Don had earlier checked all the metal fences from the far Hollymount Square entrance, to the Bell's Close entrance and all was secure. The men had pushed cars in front of the fences to obscure view into the Square.

Hannah was exhausted and Colleen put her arm around her, 'listen, you go to bed. I'll stay up with Amelia, it's ok.'

Hannah walked over to the front door and picked up her trainers, 'I've got a better idea. It's dead quiet, out there. Let's go for a stroll around the square. We can use the pushchair, we took from the house over the road, last week. It might just get her to sleep.'

The couple made their way out of the house and headed around the circuit shaped road.

There was a full moon and it reflected off the damp tarmac road, just enough to light their way.

Marty had heard the two go out and couldn't sleep, himself, so he got ready and went outside and started jogging around the Square to catch them up.

As the couple passed Don's house, Hannah held up her hand, 'stop, there's somebody walking this way.' Hannah had a shoulder bag hanging from the pushchair handle and she reached inside and pulled out a sheath knife.

Hannah took a few steps forward and called out, 'who's there?'

'It's me and I'm not happy with that one. He's a rip. I'm going over to Hilda's this time.'

It was Dot Smith and, as she approached, Hannah quickly realised she was bleeding from her arm.

Hannah ran over and put her arm around Dot. She pulled up Dot's sleeve to reveal a deep round bite. She turned to Colleen, 'Dot's been bit. It must be Lance, something's wrong.'

Colleen ran over, put the brake on the pushchair and guided Dot to a low front garden wall and sat her down. She went into the baby bag and pulled out a disposable nappy and held it firm on Dot's arm.

Dot winced with pain and continued, 'It's that Hilda Brown's kid. I'm going down there, this time. She just lives on the other end of the cut. He's the one that couldn't behave himself at the Jubilee party, scratching and biting other kids, throwing food around. He's a bad egg. Wait till I see Hilda.'

Colleen looked Dot in the eyes, 'is Lance alright, Dot? Did Lance bite you?' 'Lance? no, he bit Lance, as well, little terror. He was in our back garden pinching stuff.'

Colleen screamed after Hannah, 'Hannah! there's dead in the Square, it's not Lance.'

Hannah had just passed through Lance's front gate and she turned around and looked in horror as a young dead boy approached Colleen, Dot and the baby, from out of a front garden and stopped at the pushchair. She screamed out, 'Colleen! Amelia!'

Colleen turned and saw the boy stoop down over Amelia, but he was suddenly carried away by Marty, who had rugby tackled him around the chest, into the middle of the road.

Midgy had heard the commotion and ran out, carrying a baseball bat.

Marty was calling out in distress. He hadn't been bitten, but he was still not anywhere near fully recovered from being stabbed by Alec Donaldson and the injured area was now a source of pure agony.

The dead boy got to his knees and began to crawl towards Marty. Midgy ran over and smashed the bat into the back of the boy's head.

Sandra Mijeson ran out into the street and called over to Hannah, 'we'll check on Lance, go see to Amelia.'

By now most of the residents were at their doors and Dowser and Paul joined Midgy, heading for Lance's house. Don ran towards the baby.

Colleen was hysterical. The boy hadn't taken a lump of flesh, but there was a deep bite mark, where the top row of teeth had penetrated Amelia's right forearm and a graze underneath, that had just broken the skin, like an abrasion. But for Marty's tackle, the bite would have been down to the bone, on such a small arm.

Amelia was crying, bitterly with the pain and shock.

Hannah was in full sprint and came to a stop, when she saw Amelia's arm. She fell to her knees, alongside Colleen, who was now tending to the baby.

Don was in tears and he sat down beside Dot.

Dot looked at Don, 'hello Jack, long time no see.'

Don didn't even try to convince Dot that Jack was actually his late father. She was confused enough, without bringing her dementia into the mix. He took her arm, 'come on, Dot, let's get you back home. Lance will be worried.'

Don looked across to Hannah, 'I'll be around as soon as I can.'

Eileen Moorhouse and Clarky ran to Marty and Clarky took him in his arms and carried him back home. Hannah and Colleen arrived at the house at the same time, with the baby.

Lance was laid on the kitchen floor, when Midgy entered through the back door. The door out to the garden was wide open and he could hear bumping against the bottom fence.

Midgy knelt down beside Lance and Dowser and Paul entered the garden, making their way to the bottom fence.

Lance had lost a lot of blood. Midgy held his cold hand, 'what happened, Lance?' Lance was struggling to breathe, but managed to say, 'I heard a noise, in the garden. I went outside with a hammer, but, but it was just a little boy.

A rail had come off the fence. He'd squeezed through. I couldn't hit him, son. He grabbed me and I fell. The bite is on the back of my neck. I know I'm not going to make it; I've lost too much blood.'

Lance smiled broadly, 'God almighty, you should have seen it, though. Dot thought it was a kid from years back, a right little shit from Cornwall Crescent. She ran him off with the broom. It was something to behold. Dot, is she alright?' Midgy smiled, 'she's fine Lance.'

Lance closed his eyes and his breathing shallowed. He died a few moments later.

By the time Don got Dot inside, the bite to her arm was showing severe infection. It was dark red and she had become unresponsive, probably due to extreme pain. She hadn't 'ran the boy off,' he'd just walked away, content, when he'd taken the bite out of her arm.

Don carried Dot into the sitting room and laid her on the settee. The wound wasn't bleeding anymore, but was becoming infected so quickly, that her whole arm was purple.

Midgy walked through from the kitchen, wiping his knife on a tea towel. He looked at Don and shook his head. Don nodded towards Dot's injury and Midgy put his hands on his head. Sandra put an arm around him.

Dowser came in from the garden. He patted Don on the back, 'would you have the cordless driver handy?' Don nodded, 'it's still in the bag on the kitchen table, at home.'
Paul ran off to get it.

Dowser continued, 'there's a fence paling had rotted, just one. The dead have been around the perimeter fence on the school side. They must have pushed at every paling and this one fell in. It hasn't been enough for them to get through, but a child. Looks like he somehow managed to squeeze through.'

Don walked outside. Ronnie, Vic and Chris had done a sweep of the Square. Ronnie walked over to Don, 'the Square's clear Don, it was just the one. How did it get in?' 'they broke a weak fence paling. Ronnie, could you do me one more favour, just check all the houses adjoining Hollymount Terrace are locked down and secure. The fence along there is weak, but we boarded everything up, inside. Just peace of mind there is no way in for them.'

Ronnie nodded and the three men ran off towards those houses.

Don walked back into the house. Dot was unconscious and Sandra was knelt beside her.

Sandra pulled open Dot's blouse, revealing discolouration right across her chest. She was breathing shallower and shallower and her skin was white. Sandra looked up, 'Don, she's not got long.'

Don unsheathed a knife and the others left the room. He lifted Dot into a seated position and sat on the settee, beside her, allowing her head to lay on his lap. Don took the knife and pierced Dot's temple. He carried her outside and laid her body on the ground, at the bottom of the garden.

Midgy followed behind, carrying Lance.

Paul Dawson had arrived with the cordless driver and Dowser had found a length of timber in the garage. They quickly fixed it in place on the fence, closing the gap. They all could still hear dead, bumping against the fence in different places, but it was secure.

Paul walked over to Don, who had found a spade and he held out his hand, 'When Ronnie gets back, we'll take care of this, Don. Hannah and Colleen need you, now.'

Amelia was in Colleen's arms and Marty was laid out on the settee, when Don arrived.

Dawn was tending to Marty, but there was little she could do, other than hold his hand. His injury was aggravated internally and starting to bruise around the scar tissue.

Dawn was praying that rest would be enough for Marty to recover. They had no medical expertise. It was a small miracle he'd survived the stabbing, in the first place.

Colleen was holding Amelia, who had gone to sleep. Her arm was dressed and blood was showing through the dressing, but Amelia still had colour. Hannah couldn't speak. She just cried and lay against Colleen, who was putting on her bravest face.

It was like a vigil all night outside the house. Everyone stood, or sat silent, some had fallen asleep, sat on walls, or on the damp ground, but the residents were all outside.

It was four o'clock am when Amelia woke her two mothers, Marty and Don. They had all dozed off, a short while earlier.

Hannah quickly got to her feet, 'please tell me she's crying for her bottle.' Colleen quickly pulled a changing mat, from under the settee and laid Amelia on her back. She opened up the body grow and changed Amelia's nappy, while Hannah warmed up a bottle, in the kitchen.

Don watched on, as Colleen carefully removed the dressing. They looked at each other in disbelief, when Amelia's arm was exposed. There was no discolouration and the wound was scabbing over, with swollen, protruding tissue along the teeth marks.

Colleen called out, 'Hannah!' and Hannah came through from the kitchen. She burst into tears of joy, as the realisation hit her that her baby wasn't going to die.

Don walked outside and spoke to the residents, who were still there, 'Amelia has survived the bite, she's alive.'

Among the celebrations, Vic looked across at Dawn, who nodded, with a look of extreme concern.

When everyone was gone home, Hannah went back into the kitchen and brought Amelia's bottle through.

Colleen was still knelt on the floor, dabbing the bite with antiseptic and she quickly re dressed the wound, so Hannah could feed the baby.

As Hannah picked up Amelia, she gasped, 'Colleen, look, have you seen her eyes.'

Colleen stood up from the floor, 'no, I was cleaning her injury, I never...'

Colleen looked into Amelia's eyes. They had changed colour. They had been green, but they were now two colours, sky blue, with a royal blue circle around the outside of each iris.'

21

Sir Edwin Mcghee

As the pandemic spread rapidly through the population, the government had always 'followed the science,' but 'the science' had lost its way after the virus had mutated, causing reanimation of the dead.

They had no answers and, the establishment, from secret and secure locations, were strongly pressurising the politicians to come up with a solution.

The primary goal, at first, was to find a vaccine, that would not just prevent a bite from being terminal, but also prevent the reanimation of the dead.

Unfortunately, as the need for such a breakthrough became desperate, so did the methods used and medical ethics and moral values were soon being put aside.

At the top of society and from their safe havens, scientists, politicians and government officials pushed for human testing, but there were no potential volunteers in their ivory tower.

It was decided survivors would be rounded up and taken to centres for compulsory testing, with the aim of finding an immune survivor. The theory was, if there was immunity, the body's methods of forming antibodies could be duplicated.

Unfortunately, in the absence of any survivors that had survived an attack, the primary method of testing was to initially expose the test case to a bite and this caused a massive ethical conflict between leadership of the military, establishment and politicians.

The Prime Minister had called together all senior leadership of the army, to resolve this issue, but rather than debate the issue, all of the most senior military personnel were arrested and detained at a stronghold outside of London.

The Army had taken heavy casualties, to the extent local police were armed in last ditch attempts to save cities, all over the country. As the last line of defences fell, special ops teams, that had carried out rescue missions all over the country were called in for deployment to support the civilian testing.

Politicians were assigned groups of special forces with scientific personnel and, by Chinook helicopter, transported mobile labs around each region they had been designated, all over the country.

In time, rumour had reached politicians that some children had survived bites and the priority shifted to the search for children.

The military became murder squads, controlled by the political lead.

They would arrive, as friends at any survivor community, identify and shoot potential leaders and extract the children, for testing and this had major moral and ethical implications for the soldiers. Many were shot for refusing to comply. A good number deserted.

The politicians controlled the military through fear, not leadership, managing to keep the 'scientists' working. Just like in the political world, the scientists who were wholly lacking in ethical values had risen to the top

When the Prime Minister called ministers together for allocation, Sir Edwin Mcghee already knew his designation.

Sir Edwin had been a successful businessman in his early career days, initially buying heavily into utilities sold off by the Tory government in the eighties, then selling on, days later, at huge and obscene profit. In effect, he had signed one piece of paper to buy and another piece of paper to sell and he'd made multi millions of pounds, without a penny ever changing hands.

Sir Edwin had been on the board of numerous corporate companies and had great influence with government ministers. He was often given advanced warning of impending government spending plans and had a knack of quickly setting up a convenient company, that could 'provide' what the spending plan needed.

He was often awarded multi - million-pound contracts, without competition, or tender and, on many occasions provided nothing in return.

In return, Sir Edwin was a generous donor to the Conservative party. He had learned early in his career, that a two hundred-thousand-pound donation to this political party, could become a twenty-million-pound contract and, in his case, eventually a knighthood.

Later in life, Sir Edwin had been drawn to politics and enjoyed being part of the political world. Politics was also a great opportunity for networking and Sir Edwin had fingers in many lucrative pies, so to speak.

Sir Edwin had the prime minister's ear. He knew people and he knew the prime minister was a narcissist and pathological liar.

Sir Edwin also knew that the best way to elevate one's self in the eyes of such a narcissist is to agree with their every word and this got Sir Edwin very close to him. He became the prime minister's most trusted colleague and, as the decision making became unethical, Sir Edwin was at the side of the prime minister for every decision, every briefing and every announcement.

Sir Edwin knew his designation, when the prime minister met with politicians, that day. His designated region was north of Newcastle up to the border.

Sir Edwin had a dual interest. To seek out children with immunity, for experimentation and to find his son, who had been abandoned during the extraction of VIP's from Newcastle.

The routine was always the same. The Chinook would be landed on farmland, away from collections of dead. The farm houses would be secured and a lab set up. The ops team would establish a secure perimeter, while Sir Edwin would work with a technician, studying satellite images and sending drones over the targeted areas.

When pockets of survivors were identified, the ops teams would infiltrate and extract.

Within a few days, all surviving children would be tested, their bodies cremated and the team would move on.

Once up and running, Sir Edwin would retire to a secure room and spend most of his time at the radio, in the hope his son would reply. He also received daily briefings from the government.

On the night baby Amelia was bitten, Dawn Todd and Vic Hind had listened in on one of these briefings.

22

A Dangerous Situation

The residents of the Square had made their way home, after hearing Amelia had survived the night.

Paul Dawson and Ronnie Binns had buried Lance and Dot. They had also dragged the dead boy and buried him alongside the graves of Jimmy Donaldson and the other intruders.

The Square was quiet all day.

The kids were out in the central garden, weeding and harvesting vegetables, but many adults were lying in.

Vic walked into the garden area and watched the kids work, for a while. He called Jamie over, gave him a piece of paper and whispered in his ear.

At two thirty in the afternoon. Hannah, Don, Clarky, Midgy, Dowser, Ronnie, Paul and Chris arrived at Dawn's house. Amanda and Cynthia knocked at the door a few minutes later.

They all sat in the sitting room, some on the floor.

Vic and Dawn stood in front of the massive television.

Vic looked concerned and Dawn looked across to Hannah, 'Amelia, how is she, Hannah?' Hannah half smiled, 'she seems fine. The bite has a bright red scab over it. Apart from some bruising it looks like it will heal alright. Where the teeth had broken the skin is quite swollen. It looks like the scar will be thick.'

Hannah glanced at Colleen and Colleen shook her head. She instinctively knew Hannah was going to mention the change in Amelia's eye colour. Vic winked at Hannah, 'I'm so pleased she's survived, Hannah.'

Don spoke, 'so what's this, Vic? You haven't asked us here for nothing.' Vic looked uncomfortable, but spoke to the group,

'Dawn has been using the radio I brought, here. She's been listening in for survivors, or any activity. Last night, before…' He glanced at Hannah, 'last night we picked up a communication between Sir Edwin Mcghee and a very senior government minister, based outside London. Mcghee was reporting back from Cramlington.

I'm deeply concerned. Mcghee has a military unit at Cramlington. They have been moving from area to area, for some time now, looking for survivors.

They are setting up mobile labs for testing.' He looked at Hannah again, 'they are testing for immunity. I don't know why, but they're seeking kids, testing them in portable labs.

From what we heard; they're trying to find a child with immunity to the virus. If they do, that kid will be subject to all kinds of tests, to duplicate the immunity, find a vaccine, maybe.'

Clarky spoke up, 'they found nothing in Cramlington, where are they headed next?' Vic stood silent for a few moments, then replied, 'here.'

Dawn spoke next, 'They have identified a farm opposite Hartford Hall, Hartford Home Farm, as their next base. It will take them a few days to set up, but they land there today.

Mcghee said they would be looking at satellite and drone footage of Bedlington, within the next two days. He's targeted all Bedlington surviving children to be tested in the next seven days.'

Amanda caught Dawn's eye, 'and what does the testing entail, exactly?'

Dawn couldn't answer, but Vic did, 'unless they find an immune child, that has survived a bite, it means infecting them.'

Hannah began to cry, 'no! no fucking way are they taking my baby, no fucking way. If they're infecting kids what are they going to harvest from Amelia? No fucking way. Don, I want a gun, I want a gun, now. They'll have to go through me to get my baby.'

Don took her by the arm, 'we won't let that happen, Hannah, but you can keep a revolver, here, that's a given. I'll bring one around.'

Don looked at Vic, 'we'll fight, defend the place. They'll have a job infiltrating here and we know they're coming.'

Vic shook his head, 'I'm sorry, Don, but the first thing they'll do is blow the gates and fences.'

Clarky spoke, 'so what, then, fucking Arnie? Another one-man mission of carnage?'

Vic just looked through Clarky and around the group, 'no and we can't give up our baby, or any of our kids.

The chain of command is broken. A politician is running a military ops team, with no senior military leadership. I have to know why. I suspect the method of infecting children is to expose them to a bite.

I need to know why an ops team will let that happen. I have to isolate the ops team leader and speak with him. I know where they are going and I have the comms of the men I killed at the golf course. I'll be waiting for them and hopefully their leader will meet with me. If not, I'll take out as many as I can.'

Clarky spoke again, 'how many are there, Vic?' 'Well, Mcghee reported one deserted two nights ago and he said that left him with eleven men. They have a tech guy, a doctor and four scientists, as well.'

Don walked forward face to face with Vic, 'the men who kidnapped the Nedderton boys, led by Oliver Mcghee. Sir Edwin Mcghee is his father, am I right?'

Vic nodded. He looked around the group, 'in two days they'll know where we are. Don, you need to inform Ed at Nedderton, Harvey and Geordie. If these fuckers get to us it will devastate everything we've worked for.

I'm going out. I'll wait until they arrive, identify and establish contact with the ops lead. Hopefully he will speak with me, but if not, I will reduce their numbers.

My advice, if they come, is to fight to the last person. They'll kill some of you even if you comply.'

As the group left the house Vic took Clarky's arm, 'the next wise crack from you, I'll fucking knock you out.' Clarky nodded and turned to leave. Vic held on, 'come with me this time, Clarky.' Clarky nodded again.

Vic and Clarky made their way down to the woods, behind Beattie road. Vic was carrying a scoped assault rifle and Clarky had a revolver in a shoulder holster. He was carrying a short iron bar, that he'd found in the wash house. It was blood covered, from having smashed the skulls of the four zombies, they'd encountered on the way.

The two men walked from Bedlington Country park, along the river Blyth, to Humford, then on to the dam, around four miles.

Vic reached into his backpack and pulled out a bottle of juice, drank half and passed the rest to Clarky, 'are you sure this comes out behind Hartford Hall, Clarky?' Clarky smiled, 'we lived in these woods when we were kids, Vic. We'll come out beside a dirt track that leads alongside the fourteenth hole at the golf course. It comes out right at the entrance to Hartford Hall.'

When the two men got to Hartford Hall, Vic scanned the area around the farm houses with the rifle scope. He passed the rifle to Clarky, who took a look, 'doesn't look like they're here yet.'

The two men crossed the road and ran along to the farm entrance, passing through and onto the fields, behind. There was a field that led to some hedges around two hundred yards away and Vic could see a large house on high ground.

The two men walked over the field and around the house. There was a plaque on the front of the house, that said, 'Ewart Hill House' and the house was boarded up.

Clarky made his way towards the door and Vic called him back, 'there's a good chance they'll come here if they seek food. We'll go inland.' He pointed towards a large overgrown hedge, across the field, that was covered with brambles.

Vic and Clarky had sat for hours, eventually hearing a rumbling in the distance. The noise soon increased as the Chinook passed overhead and it landed in a field, near the farm house.

There was a flurry of activity, as ops men converged on the house, closely followed by a group in white coats.

There was rapid gunfire, as the men entered the farm house, then a number of adjoining bungalows and soon, men could be seen dragging bodies across the farmyard and onto an overgrown grassed area.

Vic was watching through the scope, as Sir Edwin Mcghee was escorted by three men, one front and one either side. In a few minutes, everyone was inside and it went quiet

Vic stood up, 'we'll follow the hedge line along until we can cross the fields out of their eyeline. That's it for today.'

Clarky stayed seated, 'what do you mean, that's it for the day, they're here, Vic.'

Vic nodded, 'yes, but there's housing further down there. There will be dead all over in a few minutes, drawn by the sound of that helicopter and the gunfire. They will go silent until the morning.'

Clarky and Vic passed over some fields and found a small wooden shack, that had been used by horse owners, for storage, before the pandemic. They broke in and made themselves comfortable.

Vic had food in the backpack and shared it out, as Clarky pulled together a couple of horse blankets he'd seen, folded on a bench in the corner. The two men shared stories, into the night about how they had come to be where they are now.

Clarky woke at first light. Vic wasn't there. There was a Twix and a carton of orange on the floor beside him and a note saying, 'stay put.'

Clarky ate the Twix and waited. He truly believed Vic would knock him out if he pissed him off again.

It was an hour before Vic returned and he quickly put down the gun and started setting up op's coms. When he had his own headset on, he stepped over to Clarky and put the other on him, 'don't fucking speak, when I turn these on.' Clarky nodded.

Vic looked in Clarky's eyes, 'three, two one' and they clicked the devices on.

They heard nothing at first, but then a voice, 'Langholme, Rix, establish safe path to the equipment.' 'Affirmative.'

There was a short pause, 'obstruction removed, safe path established.'

The voice spoke up again, 'West, Manners, Birch, green light required for offload of equipment,' 'affirmative, offload of equipment is a go. 'Langholm, Rix, commence offloading, rest of squad to the helicopter, let's get this place set up.'

Vic and Clarky had returned to the hedgerow, within view of the helicopter and could see men in black uniforms carrying equipment, guided along by people in white coats.

Everyone stopped, dropped equipment and readied weapons, when Vic spoke.

Vic took a breath and spoke into the comm, 'my name is Vic Hind, special extraction team, that was abandoned at Newcastle. I believe you are looking for my team.'

There was a silence, then the man who had been supervising the others spoke, 'Vic Hind, you are speaking to Commander Drew Chapman. What is your location?'

Vic waited a few moments, 'tell me Drew, who is listening in to this comm?' 'just my men.'

Vic paused again, 'your men and Sir Edwin?' 'I communicate with Sir Edwin by walkie. My men aren't party to discussions with the minister. Tell me, Hind, are your team safe and well? I can have you extracted, if you are nearby.'

Vic responded immediately, 'I was nearby an hour back, Drew. I had your head in my sights. You were speaking with two guards, remember? One lit a cigarette with a silver lighter, the other was wearing Adidas trainers, not regulation attire, but I suspect he has a foot condition and is unable to wear boots?'

There was a long pause, but Vic and Clarky could see the men had stayed put, waiting for instructions. Chapman spoke again, 'Hind, please tell me the status of your team and, Hind, what do you want?'

Vic could see Chapman through the scope. He looked nervous, 'I want to meet with you one to one. I have snipers on your position. If I wanted you dead, I would have pulled the trigger, earlier, so rest assured you are safe to meet with me.

Come alone. There is a stile to the left of Hartford hall entrance, across the road from your location. Over the stile, there is a footpath that leads along the edge of the golf course and into the woods.

Follow this track, alone, until you reach a large concrete dam, about a mile along. You have my word I only wish to talk, but if anyone follows you, they will be taken out by my team and I will also shoot you.'

The comms went silent and Vic watched, as Chapman looked around his team.

After what seemed an eternity, Chapman spoke, 'alright, Hind, I will meet with you.' Vic spoke for the last time, before turning off comms, 'one hour,

Drew and the minister is not to be informed, do I have your word?'

'Affirmative.'

The Realisation

Drew Chapman nervously followed the river along from Hartford woods, arriving at the agreed time at a large concrete dam. The water was deep at the top of the dam and there was a type of water flow arrangement, covered by a thick, rusted metal grating, down the side, allowing water to cascade down through five levels, then into the river below.

On the opposite side of the dam, there was a flat shallow, allowing water to flow around the far side of the dam, creating a waterfall into the river below.

There was a country path, leading into the woods on the side of the river Chapman was on and the opposite side was steep, tree covered embankment, that led to fields, above.

Chapman stood alongside the dam. He was unarmed.

After five minutes Chapman called out, 'Hind, are you here? I've come alone, as agreed.'

Vic walked out from the path Chapman had arrived from. He'd followed him since Hartford Hall.

Vic was holding a silenced revolver, but quickly holstered it and pointed to a fallen tree trunk. The two men sat down and Vic spoke first, 'thanks for meeting with me, Drew. I have no intention for conflict, here. The revolver was for anyone that followed us.'

Chapman looked Vic in the eye, 'I gave you my word.'

Vic sat quiet in thought for a few moments then spoke again, 'I don't have a team with me, Drew. I have an armed detective, who was abandoned during the evacuation of Newcastle.

He was one of the domestics left to die, by the powers that be. He is no match for your team and neither am I, alone. I know that.

We have a community in Bedlington, as you will know in a couple of days and I have been listening in to Sir Edwin's briefings with your leadership. Your leadership are politicians?'

Drew looked uncomfortable, 'We were all briefed that the leadership structure had changed. The Senior leadership in the military has been removed, Hind. We answer to the government, now. Non - compliance is a capital offence.'

Vic nodded, 'mutiny?' 'no, not mutiny. The government said they needed to take measures, that our leadership structure refused to comply with. They were relieved of duty.'

Vic nodded, 'take measures, such as human experimentation? That's why you're moving from place to place. Setting up portable labs in farm houses?'

Drew was clearly disturbed and he cast a desperate look at Vic, 'We're under orders, Hind. What are we supposed to do? Good men have been shot as deserters. God, we lost a man, just two days ago. He just ran off.

I had him in my sights and I couldn't shoot him. He was one of my team.' 'Good men have been shot by who, Drew? Their own team leaders, under orders of a politician?'

Vic gave Drew a moment to compose himself, then spoke again, 'so tell me, Drew, what's the process your team are following?'
Drew sat, head down, 'They need kids. The scientists are certain the solution lies in finding someone with immunity. They were told, some time back that there was a survivor, down South somewhere, Chester. A kid had been bitten and survived, healed up.

A team was sent to extract the subject, but by the time they got there, he'd been attacked again, this time by living and he died of his injuries. Since then, they have designated teams to seek out another subject. We're searching for any kid that is immune.'

Vic looked Chapman in the eyes, 'and so you move from place to place, across a region, infecting children, in a search for one, who resists the virus. The rest dies. Fucking Hell, Chapman, what have you and your men gotten into? Politicians aren't your chain of command. What about your own families?'

Chapman looked up, 'we were assured our families would be extracted to safety, if found.'

Vic shook his head, 'and you believe that?' Chapman looked down, 'well…'

Vic raised his voice and Chapman sat up, startled, 'Lorraine and Sam Dunn! Wife and child of Aaron Dunn, live in Ponteland. Melissa and Jennifer Hardman, wife and child of Spencer Hardman, live in Cramlington. What is the status of these four family members of two of my previous team?

Surely, if you have visited these places, as I know you have, you will have been given intel on these men's families, for extraction?'

Chapman couldn't reply. Vic continued, 'surely, Drew, you were aware there may be survivors of servicemen in these areas?' 'no.' 'Then tell me, Drew, will the death squads that turn up at yours and your own men's homes, know that your wives, kids, families aren't to be harmed? No? Drew, you've been had, mate.

How do you and your men not see what's happening here? Who will benefit from any antidote, when they eventually find what they're looking for? Do you think you and your fucking teams will be sent to vaccinate people, whose kids you have taken and murdered?

They'll not even vaccinate you, Drew, for fuck's sake. The antidote, if they come up with one, is for the fucking establishment and the politicians who speak for them.'

Chapman was in tears, 'but what am I to do, Vic? Mcghee would have me shot at the drop of a hat.' Vic shook his head, 'for God's sake, Drew, think! Shot by who? You and your men are all that's left. You're fighting unarmed civilians, when you should be freeing your leadership.

You're fighting for the enemy; Drew and they are at war with unarmed civilians. All that will be left at the safe haven will be private security, fucking bouncers.

If you and the other teams turn up in force, private security will quickly realise the two things they are working for, money and safety, are not on the table any more. They'll step aside before a shot is fired. Unless they think they're match for armed Chinooks.

Drew, there's no one left after us. We are the last line and our leaders are locked up. What's left of us should be establishing a secure place and evacuating survivors to safety.'

Chapman sat, head down with a hand over his face, 'so what do I do, Hind? Tell me, what the fuck do I do?'

Vic sat silent for a few moments then replied, 'go back, talk to your men. Step aside and let me and my friend Clarky into the farm house. Let us be the first to end some of this horror.

Do you have any means of communicating with the other teams, out of earshot of the ministers?'

Chapman sat in thought, 'yes, there may be a way. The pilots have a group radio briefing every other day. They're due one today, at fourteen hundred.'

Vic responded, 'if I take down the lab here and you communicate what I have done, through this briefing, others will follow. No one in our line of work can be happy murdering civilians, or shooting their own men and you certainly aren't.

I know there's discontent in your team, men don't desert for nothing. The others will be no different. It will just need one take down and the focus will shift towards re - establishing your leadership, but you have to get them out from where they are being held.'

Vic stood up, 'talk to your men. I will make myself visible in one hour. If you are with me give me the thumbs up. If you are not, I will be at war with you. I know I can't kill you all, but be certain, Drew, if I only kill one person, it will be you, but only if I have to.'

Drew stood up and walked off along the track. Vic ran up the embankment and returned to Clarky by way of the fields.

Vic called out as he approached the storage shed and Clarky opened the door, revolver in hand, 'how did it go, Vic?' Vic sat down on a crate, 'I don't know, I can only hope I got through.'

The two men returned to the tree line and Vic watched through the gun scope, until the hour was up. Chapman and his men had come outside and Vic walked over to the middle of the field. Chapman looked around his men, then raised his fist in a thumbs up gesture.

Vic called over to Clarky, 'let's go.'

They made their way over the field and Vic put his hand on Clarky's back. 'If this is a trap, we die, but shoot as many as you can, I'll take Chapman down.' Clarky looked straight ahead, 'no problem, fucking GI Joe.' The two men giggled like kids and Vic glanced over, 'fuck you, fucking Frank Drebin.'

Chapman walked over and met Vic and Clarky, 'my men and the crew are all outside.

Vic, the two girls in the lab, Mae Lim and Angela Han, they're under duress. The tech kid, Tim Ryder, as well.

Those three have nothing to do with what's gone on. They're doing as told, to stay alive. The weird fucker, scientist kid, he enjoys his work. He's the one who infects the kids, he's called Justin Birch.

The doctor, Roger Langholme monitors the victims, euthanises the kids, when the tests fail. Mcghee is in a study at the back of the house. Take the first left for the lab.'

Vic and Clarky entered the house and immediately heard voices from a room to the left. The door was open and Vic peered inside.

A young man was chastising a dark-haired Chinese girl just inside. 'how many fucking times do I have to tell you, Mae, two fucking sugars. It's not fucking rocket science.'

Vic looked further in. Another Chinese girl was setting up a trolley that was covered by a white sheet. She was laying out surgical equipment and a doctor was attaching a drip to a mobile stand.

Vic took Clarky's arm and nodded to the far side of the room. There was a bed set up, covered by a Perspex case. There was a zombie laid on the bed, strapped down. Adjacent to the dead man's head was a round hole in the Perspex cover, about ten inches across.

Vic held the silenced revolver up and he and Clarky entered the room. Justin Birch saw them straight away, 'who the fuck are you? get out of here, this is a no-go area for you. I'll have you fucking shot.'

Vic smiled, 'shot? You mean like this.' He pointed the gun to the side and shot the doctor through the head. Doctor Roger Langholm fell back against a wall and slid down, ending up in a seated position. He was tall, thin and bald headed and was wearing brown stay press trousers and a light blue shirt, under a long white coat. Blood poured out of the side of his head.

The two girls stood silent, terrified, as Vic turned to Justin Birch. Justin was around five feet eight inches tall. He had black hair and was unshaven. He wore jeans and trainers and a black Deep Purple tee shirt, under a long open white coat.

Justin held out both hands, 'listen, we're all here against our wishes.' Vic glanced as Mae Lim gave Justin a look of disgust.

Vic stepped forward, slapped him across the face and dragged his coat off. Justin began to cry, 'please, please, they made me.'

Vic slapped him again, 'word has it you enjoy your work, son.' 'no, no, but the research, it's necessary. We need to find the solution. I know, listen, I know the methods are extreme, but if we find that one person that's immune, just that one person, it would make the difference.'

Vic looked Justin in the eye, 'make a difference to who?' Justin looked puzzled, 'we, we just need to find one, that's all.'

Vic took hold of Justin's arm and forced it into the hole in the side of the Perspex case. The zombie bit deep into Justin's forearm and he screamed in agony. Vic pulled Justin face to face, 'you just need to find one case of immunity. Maybe it will be you, then.' He let Justin fall to the floor and turned to the girls. They were both crying.

Mae Lim was in her early twenties. She was around five feet two, shoulder length black haired and very pretty. She was wearing jeans, sandshoes and a cream top, under a white coat.

Mae Lim had been recruited from her final year of medical studies.

Angela Han was a little taller, dyed red hair, that was going back to black and also very attractive. She was wearing black leggings, flat black canvass shoes and a grey tee shirt, that looked a few sizes too big, under a white coat.

Angela had also been taken from her final year of medical studies, in fact the two had been in the same university cohort.

Neither girl spoke. Vic put a hand on both their shoulders, 'go outside, I know you are here under duress. We have a safe place and you are welcome there.'

The two girls looked at each other, nodded and ran outside.

Vic took one more look at Justin, as he left the room. Justin was lying on the ground, holding the bite injury and sobbing. The Zombie was contentedly chewing away on the large lump of flesh, on the covered bed.

Vic closed the door behind him, then walked across to the study. He knocked on the door and a voice called out, 'yes.'

Clarky opened the door and Vic walked in holding the revolver in both hands.

A young man was setting up some equipment, that was attached to a laptop, at a desk to the side of the room. Clarky looked at him, 'outside, the girls will explain. You're safe, son, we're not going to harm you.'

Tim Ryder was around twenty-three years old, but one of those guys who still looked around eighteen. He was short and thin, with longish brown, straight hair and he was wearing glasses with thin blue rims. He had black jeans and trainers on and a plain black hoody.

Sir Edwin Mcghee was sat at a desk, in front of a laptop. He was around sixty years old, wearing a grey suit white shirt, with a light grey stripe, He had a dark blue tie on that didn't really look like it matched. He had tanned skin, thick, greying hair and was clean shaven.

There was a large radio set beside the laptop and numerous wires, leading outside. They could hear the hum of a generator.

Mcghee sat up, 'how dare you enter here armed. I should have you shot. How did you get past my men?' Vic lowered the gun, 'it was easy,   I just reminded them that they are not your men.'

Mcghee folded his arms, who am I speaking to? You look familiar,' 'Vic Hind, you may have seen me on photographs with your psychopath son.' 'You were with Oliver, when…' 'when he was abandoned by people like you? Yes, but only until he tried to murder me, then I ran.

Unfortunately for your son, Sir Edwin, he continued his pursuit. You see, Sir Edwin, your son was a disturbed fucker. A man who was easily unhinged, but you would know that. It's what held him back from the future you had planned for him, isn't it?

All the rapes, murders. It must have been a real task burying all those reports, like you did. You didn't bury the report, when I knocked some fucking sense into him, though, did you? No, I was on a charge, while your murdering, rapist son walked free. That's how it goes in your world, isn't it?'

Mcghee stood up, 'how dare you, do you know who you are speaking to? I am the right hand of the prime minister and, unless you haven't noticed the Prime Minister is in sole charge of this country.

I can ruin you, boy. You mention my son. Where is he now? Tell me!'

Vic smiled, well, Sir Edwin, Oliver was attracted to me, so much so he searched the region, just for the pleasure of killing me. He kidnapped children all over, to intimidate survivors into handing me over, but I was never there. Eventually he caught up with me and now it's over.'

Sir Edwin scowled at Vic, 'you killed him?' Vic looked him in the eye, 'no, my friend Bunter did. He ate your son Oliver's face.

I killed his team though. Now I need some information from you, Sir Edwin. There's a pen and notepad in front of you there. Write down the locations of our senior military personnel, the prime minister and his cronies.'

Sir Edwin looked Vic in the eyes, 'fuck you.' Vic smiled, 'I'm refreshed to see loyalty from a man like you, but I do need the information, unfortunately for you.' Vic pulled out a knife and grabbed Sir Edwin's left, arm, holding it tight to the desk and pressed the blade of the knife hard down, removing Sir Edwin's thumb.'

Sir Edwin was hysterical, crying and screaming and Vic stood back. He waited until Sir Edwin looked up then said, 'if I have to ask you ten times, I'll have to do the writing for you. I've got all day and you also have ten toes. I'll give you five minutes between amputations.'

Vic sat at the side of the desk and took a small clock and turned it around, so Sir Edwin could see the face.

Sir Edwin held the stump of his thumb as the time ticked by and, as Vic stood up and yielded the knife a second time, he grabbed for the pen, started writing, then handed the notepad to Vic.

Vic read the locations, then passed the notepad to Clarky. He raised the revolver and shot Sir Edwin in the forehead.

Vic and Clarky walked back outside. Drew walked over and shook hands with both men.

Clarky held onto the handshake and passed the notepad to Drew, with the other hand, 'this is the location of your leadership and the other site is the safe haven of the prime minister and the elite.'

Vic spoke, 'I hope you pull the teams together, Drew and go after them. I'm confident you are the man to do it.' Drew nodded, 'come with us, Vic.'

Vic shook his head, 'I'm finished with that world, Drew. I have someone now and a small community of survivors, that need me.

No, Drew, when I saw the team turned away from that Chinook, at Newcastle, with our own side's guns in their faces, surrounded by hundreds of dead, I was finished.

The powers that be have no loyalty. My gut tells me that you're the man who can change that and I hope you do.

If nothing else, what I've done here will buy my people a bit more time, but I hope I never see military again.'

As Vic walked away Chapman called behind, 'I'll do my very best, Vic.'

Clarky stood by the three youngsters, that had been sent outside. They were all stood, heads down and terrified. He spoke to the three of them, 'listen, the soldiers have a tough task ahead. I don't recommend you go with them. We have a safe community. Come with us.'

Angela turned and spoke in Chinese to Mae and then replied to Clarky, 'we have medical equipment that may be of use to you.' Clarky nodded and took them back inside. Tim followed.

The girls completely ignored and worked around Justin, who was hysterical on the floor, sat up against a cold radiator. Tears were running down his face and his nose was running just as fast.

Clarky looked at him, as the girls packed two back packs and two large cases, with medical supplies. He smiled when Justin looked up, 'by the look of that arm, I don't think you're the immune one. Bad luck, Justin, son.'

Justin grimaced with pain. His arm was now purple and he pleaded to Clarky, 'please, shoot me.' Clarky knelt beside him, 'you know what happens, then, when they turn?

You know what it's like, how painful it is? You've watched it happen with the kids, haven't you?

Fuck you, son. It's your fucking turn now, before you go to hell. You're not worth the bullet.'

Tim had walked back into Sir Edwin's office. He stepped back in horror when he saw the body slumped face down on the desk. There was an exit wound from the back of the head, covered in brain tissue and blood up the back wall. Tim saw the amputated thumb lying on the desk, beside the body.

He quickly pulled together his laptop and drone equipment and carried it all out in a large canvass bag, meeting Clarky and the two girls on the way.

Sir Edwin's pen was in Tim's pocket. It was a very expensive Montblanc and he had just the person in mind for its next owner.

Clarky left the farmhouse with the youngsters and walked over to Chapman, 'the Justin guy's been bitten. I locked the door; in case he turns and one of you walked in on him.' Chapman looked over, 'we won't be back in there.'

As the group made their way into Hartford woods, Clarky, Mae and Vic walked together. Angela and Tim walked on ahead, hand in hand. All five were carrying heavily laden bags.

Clarky caught Mae's eye and pointed at the two. Mae smiled, 'they've been together for a while, now, in secret. They take every chance to catch a few minutes together. It's the first time they've been free together, though. I think they may need a room, when we get back to your community.'

Clarky laughed and shook his head, 'that's one thing we've got, Mae, plenty room, but one thing, though, the experiments, the research, it's over. We have two casualties back home; we could use your help with.'

Mae looked Clarky in the eye, 'all we wanted to be was doctors, Clarky, nothing more.'

Clarky smiled, 'well I'm sure we'll keep you busy, if that's the case, young Mae. By the time you add this lot to our medical supplies, you'll be able to start your own practice.'

All the residents came outside, when word got around that Vic and Clarky had returned. The group had put their bags down and were waiting for Vic to return with Dawn.

All the residents were assembled, as Vic and Dawn came outside.

Vic nodded to Clarky. He wasn't the best at public speaking and was happy for Clarky to feed back.

Clarky stepped forward and spoke, 'I'm sure you all know by now that there was a real threat coming our way. Vic managed to speak with the ops team leader and we have taken down the minister, who was leading them and a lab, where they were planning to experiment on children.

The people here, Mae Lim and Angela Han are doctors. Tim is a technician. They were being kept there under duress and I have offered them a home, here. These people, Vic and I, have carried a lot of medical supplies with us and Tim has drone technology, we can use to observe what's going on outside.'

Colleen walked over, 'I'm sorry to interrupt, Clarky, but could the two doctors be excused? Marty and Amelia...' Mae picked up a black bag, 'of course' and the two young doctors followed Colleen.

Colleen put an arm around Mae and whispered, 'I hope I can trust you. My baby survived a bite.' Mae stopped in her tracks and looked across at Angela, then back at Colleen. 'you must tell no one of this outside your community. Of course, you can trust us, please let me see.'

Outside Clarky continued, 'The special services appear to be all that's left of the military and the man we spoke to, Drew Chapman, has taken charge of the team that was a threat to this region. They are leaving.

At the heart of things and countrywide, the prime minister has taken full charge of everything and imprisoned the upper leadership of the army. Chapman now has their location and the location of the pigs responsible for what has been going on.

We are hoping the same happens all over the country and the focus of the ops teams shifts towards rescuing their leaders and eliminating any further threat to civilian survivors; people like us.

Time will tell, but we are hopeful that word will go around in a countrywide briefing, this afternoon, that there is no one available to the ministers to carry out their threats of execution of any servicemen not complying with them.

When the teams unite, they have fully armed Chinooks and black ops personnel. They will take back control.'

Dawn was stood beside Vic and she spoke, 'I'll arrange houses for the new arrivals.'

Don stepped forward, 'thank you Vic, Clarky, for what you have done for us today. You both knew that your mission was one way, if the military wouldn't listen to you and you selflessly risked your lives to give us a chance, to protect our children.'

Don looked around the residents, 'we are locked down for now. The store house is well stocked and we are harvesting vegetables.
We have chickens, ducks and rabbits and the breeding programme is working well. I want no one out of the perimeter, for any reason.

Maybe Tim can use the drones to observe the dead and give us an idea of their threat? but we must keep our heads down.

The farm, Nedderton and Breakers survivors all know the same. Autumn is just round the corner, then Winter and we don't know how the dead will respond to the cold, but if they go down again, we move and we move fast.'

24

Four Weeks of Lockdown

It was two o'clock pm and Dawn had found the channel the Helicopter crews were communicating on.

Drew Chapman had taken the comm and requested communication with all the team leaders. Helicopter crews had complied.

Vic had been right, it had only taken one minister to be taken out, for the realisation to kick in, that the people leading the atrocities had no one to implement the capital punishment, that came with non - compliance.

Across the country, depending on the team leaders, ministers, scientists and doctors were either arrested, or shot and plans put in place, to establish a base and leadership structure.

The goal was to free the military leadership and take control from the Prime Minister and establishment, but the good news was that the experimentation had stopped, countrywide.

When a base had been established, the radio communications stopped and Vic was tuning in daily, hoping for any communications from Drew Chapman. He knew he'd hear nothing until the mission was complete.

The Farm was busy. Vegetable gardens were being maintained and the animals, that had been brought in from the fields, were being kept in the large barn and needed care, daily. There were plenty volunteers for that.

There were dozens of dead, outside the perimeter. Geordie had allowed the kids to take down small groups of dead with ball bearings shot from catapults, from the safety of the tall wall of hay bales. They went silent, however, when large groups of dead appeared.
The farm was safe and the boundaries holding out.

At the Square, the two doctors had settled in and both Marty and Amelia were recovering well, with their support.

Angela and Tim had taken up residence in one house and Mae had moved into another, taking all the medical supplies and equipment with her, including what was in the store house.

Jean and Don had become close friends and Jean declined the offer of her own house.

Jean valued Don's support and both Don and Jamie liked having her around.

Bob Rice had taken up residence in his own home and he had a keen interest in growing vegetables. He was first in the central garden, every day and last to leave.

Chris Dewhirst had stayed with his sister, Margaret Hipsburn. Not that he didn't want a place of his own, but Margaret didn't like being alone, so he was happy to stay with her.

Ted Knight had lived with his daughter and the girls, for a couple of weeks, but eventually took one of the houses overlooking the park. He had taken an interest in the animals and he enjoyed building things, so spent a lot of time in and out of wash houses, as he built up a good set of tools.

Within days Ted had started building a better hen coop and he had plans for housing the rabbits and ducks. Ted spent time with Bob Rice and the kids every day, making plans and building stuff.

The friends met on a regular basis, Don, Dowser, Angie, Clarky, Eileen, Paul, Marie, Midgy, Vic, Dawn, Ronnie, Thelma, Hannah and Colleen. There was plenty drink to cater for parties, the Donaldsons house had been packed with hundreds of bottles of spirits, enough to last years.

The university girls, Honour, Julie and Sam continued baking for the Square residents. They spent most of their time together, but occasionally joined the friends at Don's place. After all, they did the catering.

Amanda and Cynthia had become more than friends. They had continued to sleep in the same bed, and often cuddled together and, one evening after sharing a bottle of Cava, Cynthia had summoned up the courage to ask Amanda if she had ever kissed another girl. Her answer was 'no, but I'd like to' and, within seconds they were kissing, getting naked and one thing led to another.

Although it was Amanda and Cynthia's secret, Hannah and Colleen knew, just by the way they were together, but they never said anything.

Amanda and Cynthia attended the parties, as well. They were always available to help out where needed and Dawn had become good friends with them. Dawn also knew about the relationship. Dawn knew everything.

Clarky had been troubled for some time. He had a good friend in Eileen and, without her, he'd have no doubt taken his own life, at his darkest ebb, Eileen was a best friend, nothing more, but they enjoyed each-others' company.

In time, Clarky began to get back to his normal self. Having so many friends helped and he spent a lot of time with Vic, exchanging black ops military and drug bust stories.

The kids were all happy. Most of them worked in the gardens, although Tim's technology and his expert ability in computer games, made him a big attraction and his daily operation of the drone, over Bedlington often drew such a crowd, he'd started showing it as a live broadcast on a big screen TV, so everyone could see.

Don communicated with Ed, Geordie and Harvey every other day and all was well.

In the fourth week of lockdown, Tim knocked at Don's door. He was carrying a laptop under his arm.

He set the laptop going on the kitchen table and turned the screen towards Don, 'I took this footage today, Don. The last few days, the dead have been tiring, slowing down. This started to happen, this morning.'

Don watched as the footage, taken from high up showed dead going to ground, some rolling on their backs, like before.

When Tim left, Don got on the walkie and spoke with Ed, Geordie and Harvey, 'the dead are going down, again. This time we need to act. In a day or so, when they are all down, we must go out and finish them all. We'll allocate a place for a mass grave.'

Everyone was in agreement. When all the dead were down, there would be mass termination and disposal. Bedlington would be cleaned up of dead.

Don walked along to the Bell's Close entrance fence and looked out. There were dead lying on the road outside and some staggering around, aimlessly. He looked up, skyward. There were birds floating around, high up. He heard loud squawks, as around ten crows landed on a roof top across the road.

25

Mark and the Others

The evenings were getting colder and darker and Mark Fitzgerald had laid low, since Eustace's visit.

Four weeks earlier, Eustace had arrived with a message from Don Mason, one of the people who had come for Hector Fisher, that day and he'd advised Mark to lay low and lock down, but that's how Mark lived, now anyway.

Mark had noticed, from observing the main road from the upstairs window of Hector Fisher's house, that the dead were again running out of energy. There were so many dead, with access to so little food and, even with the instinct to search, that they hadn't shown before, the dead were wandering aimlessly, again.

It was cold and raining outside, a typical October day and Mark was sat at a window, watching the main road, when he saw Eustace and Ed making their way towards the top barrier, carrying bags.

He untied his hair, then walked down to the barrier and stood and watched as Ed and Eustace climbed over.

Mark stood, quiet. He hadn't been in contact with any living, for some time and he was anxious and clearly nervous about making eye contact.

Ed glanced at Eustace then spoke, 'Mark, how are you, son? We noticed the dead have slowed up. I thought it was a good opportunity to call on you. We've brought you some food. There's a side of venison in the bag, here, do you have the means to cook it?'

Mark looked down and mumbled, 'a barbeque.'

Ed and Eustace put the bags down. There was an uncomfortable silence and Ed could see Mark wasn't coping well, 'Look son, I know you have difficulties around people, but we can set you up in a caravan, site it back away from people. On your own, you know? We'd respect your privacy.

But you'd be safe. Maybe in time, we could meet up, have a cup of tea together?'

Mark didn't look up, 'I, I'm sorry. I appreciate the food and stuff, but…'

Ed nodded, 'I understand, son. Don and the others keep in touch with us. They know the dead are slowing up again. A good number have laid down again, all over Bedlington, like they did before.

Don wants us all to go out and put them to rest. They have diggers that they can use for a mass grave.'

Mark shook his head, 'I, I can't Ed, Eustace I'm just going to remain here. I'm alright.' Ed nodded, 'Very well son, but you know where we are, if you need anything.'

Ed and Eustace climbed back over the barrier. As they walked off, Ed called back, 'enjoy the meat, Mark, son.' As Mark walked away, he muttered, 'we will, thanks.'

About twenty yards along the road, Ed stopped and looked at Eustace, 'did he say we will?' Eustace looked puzzled, 'I didn't hear, Ed. Sounded like a mumble to me.' Ed shook his head, 'that's one troubled boy.'

Mark took a knife and sliced the meat into steaks, then lit the barbeque outside.

Half an hour later Mark carried a tray of cooked meat inside and went upstairs to the main bedroom and set the tray down on a bedside table.

Mark sat down and took a bite of the steak and spoke, 'this is delicious, mam, a real treat.'

He held out another steak and his mother took a bite. Mark looked across the room, 'don't worry, Hector, Emily, there's plenty to go round.'

Mark's mother was dressed in a white cotton nightdress. It was bloodstained all over and she had bites to both arms and hands, like defence injuries. Her hair was long and grey and had been combed and tied back. Mark's mother was sat on a hardwood kitchen chair.

She chewed on the lump of meat, as Mark walked over to Hector Fisher and offered a bite of venison to him.

Hector had a deep injury to his neck, just one bite had killed him. He had light ginger, thinning hair, which had also been combed and he was wearing olive trousers, a cream, bloodstained shirt, slippers and a dark olive Marks and Spencer's cardigan. Hector was also sat on a kitchen seat

Hector bit into the meat and Mark sat on the bed. He picked up the steak he had cooked for himself and looked at Hector. 'Don't speak with your mouth full, Hector, it's not polite, what mum?'

Mark listened intently to the silence then replied, 'the men are just concerned about my welfare, what? You think they'll harm you? I heard them, I heard them, mam. Mass grave I heard them, but no, not for you. Not for Hector, or Emily. The three of you are fine here. I'll take care of you. The mass graves will be for the others.'

Hector had swallowed the mouthful of meat and Mark looked over, 'Hector, no, these people are not a threat to us. They only want to help. You sit there eating their food and bad mouthing them at the same time.

No, I won't harm anyone. I just want to be alone, that's all, anyway who put you in charge?'

Mark turned to his mother, 'no, mam he isn't right, I won't do it.'

Mark walked over to Emily, who was also sat on a chair. Emily was an old lady, around eighty years old. She was wearing navy bottoms with a navy pullover and had no visible bites.

Emily had fallen down the stairs, before anyone had been able to help her. Mark had found her dead where she'd fallen. He said nothing, as he passed the meat to Emily.

Mark walked to the bedroom door and looked back, 'I've got work to do, I'll be back later.

Finish the steaks yourselves. I trust these people. I know they will leave us alone; I'm not going to…'

Mark walked out and closed the door behind him.

The three zombies stood up and moved towards the tray, when Mark closed the door.

Later, Mark sat looking out of the bedroom window, over the main road, from Hector Fisher's house. He was repeatedly muttering the conversation he'd just had with his dead mother and Hector Fisher, as if having the same argument, but saying the things, now, that he wished he'd said before.

As his anxiety peaked Mark called out, 'I can't, I can't do this anymore.'

Mark took a hunting knife out of its sheath and held the blade over his wrist as he cried. He gripped the handle hard, but couldn't make the lethal cut and he put the knife down on the windowsill and looked out.

Tears were falling down Mark's face and his nose was running.

Mark looked out again, over the street outside. Lots of dead had begun to lay down, on their backs, face and hands up, just like before. Mark looked skyward and saw lots of birds gliding around, high up.

He heard loud squawking and watched around twenty crows land on a house on the opposite side of the road, then jostle for position. He shook his head and whispered to himself, 'again.'

Mark picked up the knife, sheathed it and walked into the bathroom. His heart was racing.

While he took a piss in the toilet, Mark saw a shaving mirror on the windowsill. He looked at himself in the mirror.

Mark was unshaven and thought for a moment about whether he should grow a beard.

He looked into his own eyes. They were sky blue, with a ring of navy blue around each iris.

Mark pulled his long hair to the side and looked at the scar on his neck. The bite was now a thick, protruding, shiny pale pink scar.

Mark took a bobble and tied his hair back. He wasn't expecting to see living for a while. He walked back into Hector Fisher's bedroom and lay down on the bed.

Mark soon settled down and, after a while, the anxiety subsided. He thought again about earlier.

Mark knew that the dead had no thoughts, no communication. He knew the voices he was hearing was down to his mental health condition and not the words of his mother and her friends, but he also knew there was something. Something that was enough for Mark to continue to protect them from the living.

After an hour or so, Mark went outside and spent the rest of the day further securing the barrier outside.

It still wasn't keeping people out, like it was meant to.

Mark put his hands over his face. He didn't want the mass termination of the dead to take place. What had happened was not their fault.

Mark got back up and went back to the bedroom window. He looked down at a dead man, that had laid down, earlier and he closed his eyes and concentrated. In a minute or so, the dead man moved, stood up and walked off, towards Bedlington.

Mark focussed on three more dead, laid out across the road and closed his eyes. They all stood up and walked off in the same direction.

At Breakers, Rebecca slowly got to her feet and walked over to the window. She looked out, then across to the men, who were sat chatting at the bar and called out, 'Harvey!'

Mark walked downstairs and out the front door, heading for Ridge Terrace. He stood in the middle of the main road, opposite St Benet Biscop's school entrance and closed his eyes again. Over two hundred dead got back to their feet.

Mark watched as the dead made their way into Bedlington, then he walked towards the Red Lion roundabout, at the top of Bedlington Front Street.

There were thousands of dead, down Choppington Lane, Hartford Road and the Front Street, most on the ground, now.

Mark closed his eyes and concentrated hard.

Printed in Great Britain
by Amazon

59629874R00106